Indie Bites

Enchanters & Experiments

Issue 8: November 2022

A note on language

We are a UK publication, but we accept work from authors all over the world. We retain each author's version of English as written, so pieces from US authors appear in US English and pieces from UK authors appear in British English etc.

Published under licence by Silver Sun Books.

Table of Contents

Letter from the Editor

Welcome to this quarter's issue! This time, we're thinking about enchanters and experiments. The stories we're featuring showcase exhausted student wizards, magical pest control services, vampire scientists, and more…

This issue has been so much fun to put together, not only because it's my first time at the editing helm, but also because all of our authors really ran with the themes and created something amazing. Running the gamut from fun and cosy to poignant and lyrical, all of these stories are perfect for reading on a dark winter's evening – whether you want to curl up with a mischievous magically-created cat, tackle the giant mushroom result of an experiment, or travel the land with a nervous young wizard, there's sure to be an enchanter or experiment here to capture your heart. Plus, the last story in the collection is an exclusive prequel from Josie Jaffrey's Seekers series, so whether you're already a fan of Cam and Ed, or new to the world of the Silver vampires, make sure to check it out!

It's been a busy quarter for the Indie Bites team, and one thing I'd love to introduce to this letter going forward is a bit of an update on what we've been up to as well as putting this issue together for you! I've been working on cosy fantasy short stories set in my District Witch world for the *Once Upon A Season* fairy tale anthologies from Macfarlane Lantern Publishing – these are light-hearted, queer-norm, genre-savvy takes on classic fairy tales, all with no-nonsense witch heroines, a sprinkling of romance, and terrible pun titles. I've just finished up "What Big Geese You Have", which is a retelling of The Goose Girl, and have started drafting "Far Far Awake", which is a sapphic twist on Sleeping Beauty. Josie, as well as enjoying her maternity leave, is about halfway through writing the next book in the Seekers series, *Winta's Day,* and "Bad Blood" is a little teaser for it in ways that will become clear… It's going to be twisty and turny and extremely dramatic.

And obviously, we've both been reading plenty of indie fantasy as well: I've just devoured AJ Lancaster's *A Rake of His Own,* a really fun queer murder mystery spinoff of the gaslamp fantasy Stariel series (which I adore), and *Subversive* by Colleen Cowley, which is a fascinating alternate history take on the women's rights movement – it has clever magic, sparky romance, and such a compelling plot, I read it in one sitting! Josie recently enjoyed *Snowspelled* by Stephanie Burgis, which is a sweet and romantic Regency fantasy and one of my own favourites. She says it did an incredible job of transporting her to a magical, snowy country retreat – the perfect book to accompany a hot chocolate and a cold afternoon.

So that's what we've been up to – and we'd love to hear what indie fantasy you've been loving over on our social channels! Now, let's get enchanted. There's plenty here to sink your teeth into.

Adie Hart
Anthology Editor

Next quarter's issue is *Castles & Curses*, and submissions are open now. Submissions are also now open for our May issue, *Tricksters & Treasure*. If you're an indie author or illustrator who'd like to contribute to one of our upcoming issues, then check out the submissions page on our website. We'd love to have you on board.

A note on language: We are a UK publication, but we accept work from authors all over the world. We retain each author's version of English as written, so pieces from US authors appear in US English and pieces from UK authors appear in British English etc.

Meet Author Jaime Lee Moyer

Jaime Lee Moyer writes fantasy and science fiction, herds cats, is an occasional poet, and maker of tangible things. Her first novel, *Delia's Shadow*, was published by Tor Books, and won the 2009 Literary Award for Fiction, administrated by Thurber House and funded by the Columbus Arts Council. Two sequels, *A Barricade In Hell* and *Against A Brightening Sky*, were also published by Tor. Her novel, *Brightfall*, was published by Jo Fletcher Books in 2019, and *Divine Heretic*, also published by Jo Fletcher Books, came out in August 2020. Her novelette, *Beast*, is available from Amazon, and her two indie published novels, *Youngest* and *Disposable Son*, are available from Amazon.

She writes a lot. She reads as much as she can.

Welcome to Indie Bites! This issue we're talking about enchanters and experiments, so why don't we start by talking about the magic users in your work?

I'm working on an alternate fantasy series right now about the Romanian sorcerers, wizards, mages, and a few earth witches, who live in a big colony on the northern California coast in the early 1900s. The series title is *The Lost One's War*, and it will have books set all over the state of California.

Earth witches take care of different habitats and areas across the state, and the earth. Water witches keep the rivers, the streams, and lakes healthy, ocean witches guard the seas and oceans, desert witches the huge southern desert down into Mexico, and forest witches guard the plants, the trees, birds, and animals in the woods and forests that used to cover California from the ocean to the Sierra Nevada mountains. Forest witches have a huge conflict with logging companies.

The sorcerers and high-level wizards, and even the mages, are the heroes of this book. Old world monsters followed them to California more than a hundred years before these stories take place, found a big empty land full of places to hide, and breed, and defenceless people who didn't know to be afraid. The sorcerers and wizards stand between the monsters and humanity. They also police other magic uses outside the colony, and keep them from abusing their power.

As a hybrid author, you have some books traditionally published, and some self-published. Why did you choose self-publishing for some of your work?

I didn't write the books I've indie published with the goal of putting them out myself. The second book I indie published, *Disposable Son*, was the book my first agent fell in love with and it made the rounds of all the publishers, and a few editors seriously considered buying it. I love *Youngest* with all the love, but I was told the book wasn't what publishers were looking for, so I put it out myself. I'm not sorry either.

What does your typical self-publishing process look like?

Both the books I've self published were finished and titled before I got into actually publishing them. I'm lucky in the people I can call my friends. One friend, J. Kathleen Cheney, is an amazing cover designer, and she did the covers for both of my books. I smile every time I see the cover of *Youngest*, because it's absolutely perfect for the story and the world. Another friend, Scott Coatsworth, did the formatting for both books, which is also perfect.

If you were an enchanter, what kind of magic would

you specialise in?

As I said in the first question, the world I'm writing about now has magic users called forest witches, who use a special kind of magic called earth magic to keep giant redwoods and ancient sequoias healthy and thriving. I'd love to be a forest witch, keeping the trees and animals and the birds healthy.

Have you read any good indie fantasy lately?

Two of my favorite indie fantasies this year are *A Little Too Familiar* by Lish McBride and *Good Neighbors* by Stephanie Burgis. I've read all Stephanie's adult romantic fantasy and her books keep getting better and better. I loved *Good Neighbors,* even if I can't put all the reasons into words. Books about characters finding where they belong, as well as the person they belong with, always work for me. Lish wrote a wonderful love story in *A Little Too Familiar* about Louise, an apprentice animal mage, and Declan, a wolf shapeshifter, that made me melt. While melting, I still laughed so hard it hurt. I can't recommend these two books highly enough.

What are you working on at the moment?

I just finished restructuring, and rewriting two books. The first book is called *Damien Rude, Reformed Pirate,* and I'm querying the book right now. The second book I just finished rewriting a few days ago. The book is called *Amends*, and it's the first book in the sorcerers' series I spoke about. I'm fine tuning the query letter and gearing up to write the synopsis. Cross your fingers an agent falls in love with one or both of these books!

We certainly will! Thank you so much for joining us!

Short Fiction

The Exsparrowment of Evander Hale

Adie Hart

Evander Hale, Third Star Enchanter, was going to fail his exams. He knew this fact the way he knew that trees were green and dragons were bitey, and the way he absolutely didn't know any of the billions of things he was about to be tested on.

It wasn't that he wasn't good enough – in his entry examinations four years ago, he'd achieved the highest mark ever given to an incoming enchanter – and it wasn't that he hadn't tried. It was just that revision didn't seem to *work* for Evander. He either knew a spell or he didn't. Most of the time, he was able to breeze through classes with creativity and talent, and he'd acquired quite a reputation for being top of the class; in the end of year exams, though, the ones that decided who made it to the elite Second Star and who was doomed to remain some village's hedgewizard for the rest of their lives, talent took a back seat to memory. You couldn't pizzazz your way through a multiple choice paper.

Evander sighed a sigh that made the fat candles on his desk gutter, shoving the thick spell tome away across the desk. Pieces of parchment fluttered down in all directions. He swore. Felicity had spent hours helping him make those notes, and he didn't like to think about the lecture she'd give him if she came in and found them all over the floor. *Felicity* didn't have any trouble with revision, Evander thought bitterly as he sank to his knees and began to gather up the notes, then checked himself. It wasn't worth being jealous of Felicity. It would be like being jealous of the sun for being hot, or a sea serpent for being a good swimmer. It was quite simply a fact of life that Evander's best friend was brilliant. He'd eat his silver-embroidered, pointed hat if he didn't see Felicity become First Star of the Scholarium before she was forty.

Assuming the current First Star, Tobias Prendergast, was good enough to pop his clogs in a timely manner. It seemed likely. The man was a hundred if he was a day.

One of the notes had drifted under Evander's bed, and as he stretched to scoop it up, his fingers brushed the leather binding of a book. Finding random books in every nook and cranny wasn't an unusual occurrence in a wizard's room, but when Evander pulled this particular book out, a bolt of sudden hope flashed through his mind. This wasn't just a mislaid copy of *Advanced Alchymical Analyses* or *Horology for Halfwits,* oh no. This was the workbook Evander had shoved away sometime in his second year, when he'd been reprimanded in front of the whole year group by

Professor Morgan for daydreaming – "scrying involves staring into the *magical* distance, Mr Hale, not gazing gormlessly out of the window" – and decided (not for the first time) to really apply himself to his studies.

This was the workbook filled with Evander's experiments.

Every young wizard dreamed of inventing a new spell, something that would get their names put down in the history books and textbooks alike, before they realised that there was a good reason that new spells were such a big deal – pretty much everything that would work had already been invented. There was a rumour, in fact, that the inventor of a new spell of "significant benefit to the Scholarium or the queendom" would enjoy all sorts of honours, most notably bypassing their years of study and being shot straight to Second Star status. It was a regular sight in the first few weeks of winter term, students rushing to the library clutching armfuls of scribbles, only to return dejected when they realised that Orinoco the Great had in fact already come up with self-heating socks some five hundred years ago.

While Evander might have put his sheaves of experiments away and made sure to pay attention to Professor Morgan's droning declamations, he'd never really managed to stop thinking about new spells, even if he didn't do anything with them. Magic was just so *interesting,* and there were so many different things to learn that had nothing to do with classes, and Evander's brain seemed to enjoy nothing more than jumping from thought to thought, collecting seemingly random information and making it go *ping* into something clever. Ideas were definitely Evander's strong point. It was just putting them into practice that was a pain.

This particular idea, though, began to coalesce in Evander's mind. What if there was something worth using in these idle scribblings? What if he really *could* bypass the exams and join the Second Star by creativity alone?

Some hours later, the candles on Evander's desk were mere flickering stubs and only the glimmers of stars filtered through his tiny window. He rubbed his eyes – for what must have been the four hundredth time, given how much it hurt – and leaned back to massage his aching neck with an enormous grin on his face. This one was promising, really promising.

A Spell to Turn Oneself Into a Raven, the top of the page read in handwriting spiky with excitement. If Evander could pull it off, this would be revolutionary. No one had managed to achieve human-animal transformation in six hundred years; shapeshifting was mentioned in the Histories of Illorotus, but the spells (if they'd ever really existed, given Illorotus's tendency to outright make up things like giant gold-eating ants) were lost to time. Evander was pretty sure that if he'd done the calculations correctly, he'd accounted for all the transmogrification elements and matter inefficiencies, and this might really be it. Okay, it was more of a *re*-invention than a truly new spell, but Illorotus had never specifically mentioned a raven, and Evander was ready and willing to argue the point.

Surprisingly, the ingredients for the liquid element of the spell itself were fairly basic stuff, the kind of thing any final year enchanter would already have in their ingredients chest: alder bark for the power of the wind, phoenix eggshell for rebirth, and wyvern oil for camouflage. As the dry ingredients met the wet, the mixture turned a murky purple that made Evander deeply glad he wouldn't be drinking it. After a moment of thought, he added a pinch of powdered cherry. It wouldn't hurt to have a little extra oomph.

While the potion bubbled in the copper cauldron, he wiggled off his woollen socks and tucked a calendula flower between each toe. The final step was to speak the incantation he'd devised and anoint his extremities with a potion-dipped raven's feather – oh, yes, he'd better get the feather ready. Wobbling carefully on his heels to the chest so as not to dislodge any flowers, he opened the leather roll where he kept feathers and scanned through the labels: griffin, owl, rooster... there, raven. Evander's heart sank. The raven pocket was empty. No, wait, there was one raven feather left, tucked in the bottom of the chest. Evander made a mental note to restock, then, hearing the echo of Felicity's voice in his head saying his name in a warning tone, made a physical note too.

He took out the raven feather and eyed it suspiciously. It was very small. It seemed rather ridiculous that such a tiny feather could be the linchpin of such an important spell, but Evander dismissed the thought, eager to get on. If this worked, he could make sure to get an appropriately dramatic-looking feather for the official demonstration.

He coated the feather with the purple goop, then applied it to his fingers, feet and forehead, murmuring the incantation as he went. The magic took, and Evander had just enough time to pump his fist in the air before he was overtaken by a purple swirl that spun him into dizziness.

When he opened his eyes, the first thing he saw was his beak, sitting awkwardly in the centre of his vision. Evander crossed and uncrossed his eyes, but couldn't shake it. He supposed it would just take a while to adjust. You sort of tuned out your own nose, didn't you? Maybe it would be the same for a beak. And then it clicked: the spell had worked.

Flapping his arms – wings – experimentally launched Evander up to the top of his workbench, which suddenly seemed terrifyingly far away from the floor. He'd thought ravens were quite big birds, but everything around him seemed even more enormous than he'd expected. Eager to see his success for himself, he hopped around the still-bubbling equipment, then froze as he came face to face with his reflection in the copper cauldron.

He wasn't a raven.

Where he'd hoped for imposing black feathers and a wickedly sharp beak, he saw instead a tiny, speckled brown and white body and a face that could only be described as cute.

No, he wasn't a raven. He was a sparrow.

Evander opened his mouth to curse, but all that came out was a rather pathetic-sounding chirrup.

Somehow, he'd got something wrong; he'd messed it all up again.

Okay, he needed to breathe, which was surprisingly difficult with his little bird lungs. He'd planned ahead, written out a counter-spell. He just needed to flap over to the desk, find his notes and – oh, shadows and darkfire. It was all squiggles. And not in the "Evander needs to put more effort into the presentation of his work" way. Worse.

It turned out birds couldn't read.

Evander flew wildly through the dormitory halls, slowing only as he reached Felicity's room. Her door was closed and there was no response when he perched on the handle and hammered the door with his beak, because of course, Felicity never needed to stay up until dawn revising and was probably perfectly comfortably asleep with no notion of the distress her best friend was in. Evander chirruped blasphemously. How was he meant to get in now? The dormitories were at the top of the tower, and it wasn't like he could climb up to her window–

Oh. Yes. Wings.

Evander shot out of the nearest window and counted his way around to where Felicity's window stood ajar. He'd often teased her for needing a constant breeze (she found the summers in the southern queendom unbearably hot compared to her snow-capped home), but as he slipped in through the gap, he swore he'd never again complain about the draught.

As he'd suspected, Felicity was asleep, looking

more peaceful than anyone who had a fateful examination looming had any right to be. A sudden thought flashed into Evander's mind: this wasn't a curse, but it *was* an unwanted transformation. Maybe an old-fashioned solution might do the trick?

He flapped his way softly over to Felicity's sleeping form, hovering for a moment above her face, then dropped down and pressed his beak against her lips in his best approximation of a kiss before he could talk himself out of it.

There was a shriek, and Evander's vision went white.

Unfortunately, the sudden blankness wasn't the tingly, fizzy feeling of a spell being undone, but the altogether more solid *thumpf* of a pillow to the face. And body. Evander decided very quickly that he liked flying a lot more when he was in charge of his own trajectory. He smacked into the wall and slid to the floor.

"Oh, Lady of Snows, is it dead?" cried Felicity, hurrying over. "I'm sorry, little bird, you frightened me!" She scooped him up into her hands, and Evander wince-cheeped.

Murmuring apologies and general comments on his adorableness, Felicity ran her fingers over Evander's wings and body. "Nothing broken, little one," she said, moving to the window. "Let's get you back outside."

"No!" shouted Evander, but it came out as a series of piping notes. He hopped out of Felicity's hand and over to the door.

"Well, you can't stay in here," she said with a

laugh.

"Peep peep *peep*," said Evander. Oh, how was he going to get anywhere if he couldn't speak to her?

As Felicity approached, hands out ready to scoop him up, Evander flapped over her shoulder and took refuge on her bookshelf, tucking himself in between a leather-bound tome and a thick white linen-covered book he didn't need to be able to read to recognise as the dreaded Enchanter's Examination Code. Something went *ping* in his mind.

Pulling frantically at the Code with his beak, he managed to wiggle it out until it fell onto the floor with a smack (prompting another quiet shriek from Felicity). He pushed the cover open and jumped up and down on the first word of the title page until Felicity crouched down and looked at him more closely.

"Ah," said Felicity. "*Magic* bird."

Close enough, Evander thought, cheeping in agreement. Good old brilliant Felicity. He wasn't sure he'd have cottoned on that quickly himself.

"Then what do you need from me? It's very early," she said, yawning. "I have exams next week, you know."

If sparrows could roll their eyes, Evander would have. Instead, he hopped onto Felicity's shoulder and took hold of a strand of hair that was coming loose from her braid, using it to tug her towards the door.

"Okay, I'm coming, I'm coming," she protested, laughing. Evander had never been more grateful for his best friend's no-nonsense nature. Trust Felicity to take it in her stride when a magical bird divebombed her and dragged her off somewhere unknown.

He led her down the corridors to his room, where the door still stood ajar, and as soon as she stepped inside, she gasped.

"Lady of Snows, it looks like a hurricane's been through here. Van, you idiot! How many times do I need to tell you to turn your cauldron off when you go to bed?" she said, hurrying over to do just that. She whipped the covers off the bed, but of course, found nothing but the usual mess of books, cushions, and clothes strewn underneath.

Evander cheeped from the workbench. Felicity whirled on him.

"Where's– Oh, *Evander.*" There was a wealth of different meanings in that one simple word, from worry to disapproval to grudging admiration. "You turned yourself into a sparrow?"

Evander was very glad birds couldn't blush, but he did feel an irrational urge to bury his head under his wing until the embarrassment passed. He hated to admit failure.

"And now you're stuck, aren't you? Oh, wait – let's have one cheep for yes, two cheeps for no, and three for "ask something else". Can you manage that?"

"Cheep," said Evander sulkily.

Felicity was as much a force of practicality as Evander was of chaos. Within minutes, she navigated enough of Evander's chirrups to find his notebook, and it wasn't long before the cauldron was bubbling once again with the counter-spell's ingredients.

"There," said Felicity, pouring the pea-green

mixture into a shallow dish and blowing on it. Wisps of crackling steam rose from the surface. "You just need to hop in here and get yourself all coated in the potion, and I'll do the incantation. Just try not to get any of it in your mouth, okay? I've no idea what's poisonous to sparrows and I do *not* want to have to explain your missing body to Prendergast. Ready?"

Evander did as she asked, sinking into the dish. It felt amazing – bone-warmingly comforting – like the best bath he'd ever had. And it smelled *delicious,* like berries and blossom in full bloom. He barely even heard Felicity speaking the incantation as he ruffled his feathers in glee. He dipped his head under and abandoned himself to his bird instincts, taking a big sip of potion just as Felicity finished the spell.

A green swirl rose up around the bowl. Felicity cried, "Evander, I said don't–"

Evander squeezed his eyes shut and braced himself for a repeat of the transformation's dizziness, but after a long moment, all he felt was a slight *pop*, as if his ears were adjusting to new pressure. He cracked an eye open. Felicity was still enormous. And that beak was still sitting slap bang in the middle of his vision. Still a bird, then.

"Shadows and darkfire," he said disgustedly, and it wasn't until Felicity snorted that he realised it hadn't come out as a cheep. The counter-spell must have restored his voice, but not his human form.

"Oh, Van, it *is* you," Felicity said. "When it didn't take, I was worried I'd just anointed some random bird for no reason."

"No," Evander said gloomily. "It's me all right. My raven spell went wrong. And apparently my counter-spell was rubbish too."

"Evander Hale," said Felicity in that warning voice he knew so well. "Are you seriously complaining that you turned yourself – and can I remind you that an animal transformation hasn't been done for centuries and in fact possibly has *never* been done – into the *wrong kind of bird?"*

It transpired, under Felicity's examination, that the feather Evander had used for the spell had in fact been just as suspiciously small as he'd first thought. Evander swore never to go back to that nice cheap supply shop in Brakebridge.

"Honestly, Van, it's not even dyed well," Felicity said, holding it up to the light. "Have you ever actually seen a raven? They're not exactly dinky little birds, you know."

"Of course I have," said Evander. "I was just… eager to try it out." He would have stuck his tongue out at Felicity's scoff if he could have worked out how to do it with a beak. "Can we go back to the part where you were praising my phenomenal genius in inventing a new spell?"

Felicity rolled her eyes, but couldn't hide her smile. "Right. Well, Mr Phenomenal-Genius-I-Just-Worked-Out-How-To-Skip-My-Exams, what's next? We should tell Prendergast, but *I* don't want to be the one to wake him up before dawn." They'd both learned early on in their time at the Scholarium that it was better not to accost, ask any questions of, or even attract the attention of First Star Prendergast before his third cup of tea. "So what do we do until then?"

"We turn me back," Evander said.

"What?"

"We turn me back. Now that I know it works, I'm not wasting the perfect moment, my one chance to shock everyone into realising I'm actually a great enchanter, on *this.*" He gestured at his tiny speckled body with one wing. "We turn me back and then go and buy a proper raven feather and I can demonstrate the spell in its full glory tomorrow. And anyway, it'll go better if I can transform back at will. No one wants a spell that you can't undo."

"But how? Your counter-spell didn't work," said Felicity.

"We'll just have to come up with something else. Come on, Fliss, please?" He let an ounce of wheedle into his voice. "You're going to ace these exams, we both know that, but there's no way I'll pass. And I need to show them properly that it doesn't matter if I can write stuff down, that I'm good enough as I am. Imagine Professor Morgan's face when a great big raven swoops down all dramatically over his head. It just wouldn't be as fun as a sparrow. Please?" When she hesitated, he hopped up onto her hand and added, "I'll credit you in the write-up?"

Felicity spluttered. "Evander! I can't believe you'd even think about *not* crediting me when you know I'm going to have to help you write the damn paper anyway!"

"So you're helping?" he asked, cocking his feathered head.

"Of course I'm helping," she said with a grin. "This is the most exciting thing we've ever done."

Actually, it turned out to be a fairly tedious way to spend the early hours of the morning. Evander had to restrain himself several times from nipping Felicity as she muttered half-finished thoughts under her breath too quickly for him to catch them. They'd exhausted the contents of Evander's notebook quite quickly, and had moved on to running through the known effects of every spell component they could remember (quite a lot, as it turned out, after four years of endless study). Felicity was keeping a list of anything that seemed useful, though it was incomprehensible to Evander's avian eyes, and the cauldron had been bubbling non-stop with potions and decoctions of various colours. Nothing had worked.

When the fourteenth experiment failed, Evander hopped down from the edge of the cauldron where he'd been balancing to drop individual dried narcissus petals in as Felicity stirred, and swore.

"Ironically," Felicity said, "this is really great revision."

"At this rate I'm going to need it," Evander sighed. "We've tried everything."

A strange gleam came into Felicity's eyes. "No, we haven't," she said, scooping him up in one cupped hand. "An impossible spell needs an improbable solution. Hold still." She swooped closer and laid a resounding kiss on his beak.

Felicity and Evander had kissed once before – well, twice if you counted earlier that evening, which Evander was definitely inclined not to – at the Midwinter Ball in first year, giggly on too much cider and giving in to their classmates' mistletoe pressure. That had been before either of them had realised their tastes lay in different directions, and then, as now, Evander had to suppress the childish urge to laugh and wipe his mouth with the back of his hand. Or his beak with the back of his wing, he supposed. It was just so *strange.*

"Oh well," said Felicity. "It was worth a shot. Still better as friends, apparently."

Evander swatted her with a wing. "It was *not* worth a shot, for four very good reasons!"

"Only *four*? Given the literal seconds since it happened I thought you'd have at least twelve."

Evander ignored her. "Firstly, it might have passed you by, but neither of us is exactly a princess."

"I have been wondering where my tiara was–" Felicity began, but Evander cut her off, holding up one wing imperiously.

"Secondly, this isn't a curse. Unfortunately, it's entirely my own doing."

"Yes, but–"

"*Thirdly,*" Evander said, fixing her with a beady eye, "I think everyone would be extremely disappointed if it somehow turned out I was your true love instead of Emily, you know, your *actual girlfriend.*"

Felicity reddened. "I don't know, I thought maybe a

best friend kind of love might count for something!"

"Well, obviously not in the eyes of magic," Evander huffed.

"Fine," said Felicity. "All fair points. And fourthly?"

Now that he thought about it, Evander wasn't sure he wanted to admit to Felicity that a kiss had been his first thought, too. "Never mind fourthly."

"Van…" Felicity folded her arms and narrowed her gaze. It was incredible how much admonishment she could put into a single syllable. Funny, she was much more believably menacing now he knew she could bat him across the room.

"Fourthly, I already tried it," he muttered.

"You– that was what that was?" she laughed. "When you divebombed me while I was sleeping? I thought you were attacking me! Oh, that's hilarious. Look at you all high-and-mighty about my idea, and you tried the very same thing!"

"I was panicking!"

"Evidently! Maybe you should go and divebomb *Lucas Hendry*," she said, giving the name a teasing sing-song tone. "Though I'm not sure if just mooning over him for three years quite counts as true love."

"Lucas *cannot* see me like this," Evander said quickly, hot with embarrassment at the very idea of appearing as something as unromantic as a sparrow in front of the dark-haired Second Star enchanter. "Fliss, I swear if you–"

"Keep your feathers on! I'm just brainstorming. You're right, though. We've tried everything else you've got. That last potion was close, but no click – we need something powerful."

"Griffin teeth would be perfect. Or a fire opal, if we could get our hands on one," Evander said.

"Are you sure you don't have any lying around somewhere?"

"No, Felicity," said Evander patiently, "because I'm not the queen." His Third Star equipment budget just about stretched to lumpy bits of fluorite; fire opals were rather out of the question for regular studies. Getting his hands on the good stuff was one reason he was so keen to make it to the next rank.

"And here I was bowing to you every morning." She paused for a moment. "Wait. Bowing."

"Oh no," said Evander, shaking his head in horror. "I know that face."

Felicity grinned wickedly. "Who do we know who *definitely* has a fire opal?"

Shadows and darkfire, she wanted to steal First Star Prendergast's cravat pin.

It was funny, Evander reflected as he flew down the corridor behind his best friend, how often "Felicity, no" seemed to turn into "I'd love to do that, Felicity" between his mouth and her ears.

People (naming no Professor Morgans) often assumed it was the easily-distracted Evander who was behind the majority of the trouble the pair got into, but behind Felicity's bookish nature lurked a deep well of mischief. It was just that her reputation as a perfect student meant people never thought her capable of, say, hiding a realistic replica cockatrice between the shelves in the stacks to distract the librarians while she and Evander sneaked a peek at a restricted grimoire. If there was something either of them needed for their studies, Felicity really saw no reason why something so ridiculous as rules should stop them getting it.

Which was why Evander was on his way to the dining hall to steal the cravat pin from under First Star Prendergast's very nose.

"It'll be fine," Felicity insisted. "It's not like anyone will recognise you, and you have the perfect form to just swoop in, grab it, and swoop back out. He might not even notice!"

Evander was pretty sure he'd notice. Prendergast was incredibly proud of that pin, and with good reason: a fire opal was one of the best magical amplifiers that existed, and suitably expensive to boot. The one Prendergast wore was no bigger than Evander's littlest fingernail, but had probably cost more than even a semi-decent hedgewizard would earn in five years. Evander couldn't remember an occasion when he hadn't seen that red glimmer peeping out from the First Star's neck, a potent symbol of his power and general impressiveness.

Getting into the dining hall was easy. The huge doors stood open throughout the day, and even this early in the morning, there was a steady trickle of people slipping into the room for breakfast, which Felicity joined. No one noticed a small sparrow flying in and perching on the wooden Scholarium crest that dominated the far wall, above the top table where the elite enchanters sat.

Evander peered down at the sleepy array of high-ranking heads below him. He'd never seen most of his fellow enchanters from this angle before (barring the half-dwarven Professor Gwynn) but it wasn't difficult to pick out the First Star, seated as he was in his customary gilded chair in the very centre of high table. Even from above, the opal pin winked and gleamed from his snow-white cravat. All Evander had to do was snatch it. That was all.

Across the room, Felicity contrived to drop her tray in the most dramatic way possible, sending plates and cups smashing to the ground. The resulting clatter, and the yelps of her tablemates, drew everyone's attention, just as they'd planned, and while Prendergast did little more than look up and roll his eyes, it was enough of a distraction for Evander to dive down, duck under his chin, and – there – grasp the pin in his beak.

It came loose surprisingly easily, and Evander's heart soared to match his wings as he flapped up, up, out of the reach of the unwitting First Star with the opal pin clutched firmly in his… lips? No, wait, that wasn't right.

Evander's vision filled with wisps of pea-green smoke as the magic overcame him. He pumped his wings harder, but something felt very wrong with them, and he couldn't–

Evander plummeted, landing with a *smack,* all four fully human limbs flailing, in the prodigious lap of First Star Prendergast. The opal. It must have triggered the residue of one of the counter-spells they'd applied when he touched it – unheard of, but certainly possible. That had fascinating implications for the application of delayed magic – but no, Evander could think about that if he managed to survive the next few minutes.

"Sorry, sir," he said sheepishly, holding out the pin and bracing for the incoming tirade. "I think this is yours."

There was a collective intake of breath from the room as Prendergast turned several interesting shades of puce. The old enchanter spluttered wordlessly, and Evander's heart lurched. Enraging the First Star into a fatal apoplexy was *not* the way he wanted to go down in the history books. Although at least he probably still wouldn't have to sit his exams if he was being carted to prison.

It wasn't until the table started to shake that Evander realised the First Star was laughing, great belly-deep guffaws that had the man gasping for breath.

"Hale." Prendergast wiped a tear away from his face. "Of course. Who else would choose to demonstrate a full corporeal transformation in the middle of my breakfast plate?"

"Er," said Evander nervously. "Sorry."

"Sorry?" boomed Prendergast. "You're *sorry*?"

"I know it's hardly enough to make up for all of this, but I truly am sorry, and I'll take any punishment you choose, of course, only please allow me a small delay to write-up these results as I think they–"

"Hale."

"Yes, sir?"

"Do shut up." The First Star looked around the table

at his breakfast companions. "What was it," he asked them, "a blue tit or something?"

"A house sparrow, I think," said Lucas Hendry from the end of the table.

Oh, shadows and darkfire, Lucas had seen him. Evander's ears went hot and he desperately wanted to shove his head under a wing. He settled for shrinking into himself, which drew Prendergast's attention back to him.

"A good choice, boy. Common little bird like that, practically invisible. That could be invaluable for reconnaissance and intelligencing. Turn the tide of wars, even."

Evander blinked. Prendergast *liked* the sparrow? "Er, yes, sir, exactly my thoughts. Though of course, the theory could be applied to other birds. Ravens, perhaps." He tried to make it sound like a casual thought.

"Pshaw," said Prendergast. "What good would that be? So large, so showy. No, your first idea was better, stick with that."

Well then.

Prendergast was still talking. "Is it replicable? Do you have notes? I see your examinations, boy. I know what you're like. All spark and no sausage."

"Yes, sir," called Felicity from her pile of broken crockery. "We'll have a full write-up with you by the end of the week." Evander flashed her a look of alarm, but she just grinned at him, mouthing "You did it!"

"Ah, Moore. I should have known you'd be involved in this. Very well, come up here," said

Prendergast, and as Felicity came closer, he smiled. "Pending my full approval of their report, Mr Hale and Miss Moore are formally invited to join the ranks of the Second Star with no need for further examinations."

Felicity shrieked in joy. Evander wholeheartedly agreed, but somehow managed to confine himself to an effusive "Thank you very much, sir," and a smile that threatened to split his face. Lucas Hendry shot him a thumbs up from the end of the table, and Evander felt like he might just burst with pride.

"Yes, yes," said Prendergast. "Congratulations, indeed. But Second Star Hale?"

"Yes, sir?"

"Get out of my lap. And get yourself some breakfast. You look awful."

Evander Hale, Second Star Enchanter, grinned as he scrambled down and took a seat at high table.

Adie Hart is a lover of stories and the words behind them. With a background in the history and literature of the Ancient World, and an abiding love of classic fairy tales, she writes everything from fun fantasy adventures to dark mythological retellings.

Count Tiberius the Third

Claudie Arseneault

The first time Count Tiberius the Third – full name required – leaped onto his dusty tome, Nevian startled. He had been deep in concentration, his brow furrowed as he deciphered rune patterns and the explanatory text nearby. His heart raced at the sudden blur of brown fur, and he picked up the massive feline to set him back on the ground. He didn't have time for the Count's nonsense. Master Sauria wanted to practise transmutation tomorrow and its more elaborate principles escaped Nevian.

Count Tiberius, however, did not care for his failing grasp of magic. He hopped right back onto the desk and plopped himself down before Nevian could so much as cry out in protest, stretching his legs out to their full length – and Count Tiberius the Third was no ordinary cat. Created by Master Sauria's own mentor, the feline reached a solid three feet in this position and his thick, lush coat covered the entirety of the book pages. He turned his exposed belly towards Nevian and twisted his head around to turn large, expectant orange eyes at him.

"I am not petting you."

Nevian scooped him up once more, but this time he dragged the cat all the way to the door, hands under the animal's armpits, his poor arms strained by the effort. Count Tiberius's legs slid across the ground, and Nevian almost tripped himself with them. He deposited the big cat outside then closed the door with a huff.

He had moved from the Academy and into Master Sauria's home to escape the constant noise of other apprentices, often noisily gossiping about their obsessive crushes and latest sexual exploits – often with far more details than Nevian ever cared to learn, or would ever understand. He'd not expected to gain an even more bothersome, if less confusing, study companion.

A weight thumped against the door – Count Tiberius bumping his forehead to signify his discontent, no doubt. Well, that was his problem. Nevian had runes to dissect and comprehend.

He settled down in his chair again and roamed the page, trying to remember where he'd been before the interruption. No further thump at the door distracted him. Count Tiberius must have elected to seek his actual owner for his neediness. Nevian breathed in deeply, washing away his latent irritation, and set back to work.

Count Tiberius the Third – a plague upon his name – jumped onto his shoulders, claws digging into them, and then onto the book again. Nevian hissed at the unexpected pain, and in the time needed to touch his hurt shoulder, the accursed cat had circled the pages twice and settled into a ball. He rested his triangular head on his paws and stared at Nevian, eyes half-lidded. A challenge.

"How did you even get in? I closed the door!" Nevian huffed and grabbed him again, ignoring the plaintive meow of protest, then brought him outside a second time. "Stay there. Or go bother someone else!"

Count Tiberius simply sat upon his haunches as Nevian slammed the door shut. He returned to his seat, but not to his book. The door had been closed, he was absolutely certain of it, and however Count Tiberius had snuck his massive body in, Nevian intended to find out. He prayed Sauria's mentor hadn't magicked teleportation abilities into a giant cat. Surely not. Surely not even the most extreme of cat lovers would be so foolish as to grant these little devils unlimited access to the whole world. Then again, Myrian wizards were not best known for their propensity to ask themselves whether they should try the latest feat of magic to cross their brains.

A cold sweat broke over Nevian's nape as the thought wormed its way through his mind, but before it could grip him fully, a thin golden line appeared on his door. It spread, tracing a square in the middle and bottom, thickening into hinges at the top. Those spun, and the perfect cat-sized panel flipped inward, allowing Count Tiberius the Third to strut in with his head high.

Relief at the absence of teleportation quickly gave way to irritation. A magical cat trapdoor? No wonder closing the door had no effect! Had Master Sauria installed these everywhere in the house? Nevian had only lived here for three weeks, and he'd spent a great deal of that time in his room, and now that he thought of it, he'd never heard Count Tiberius scratch or meow at any doors. He'd never questioned it, as Count Tiberius's interest in Nevian and his books was very recent, but now… He sighed as the big cat hopped right back onto his desk. This was going to be a problem.

For the third time, Nevian carried him out of the room. This time, however, he collected every thick tome he owed and piled them in front of the magical panel. He doubled the thickness before bookending the set-up with extra-thick books and standing back. Hands on his hips, Nevian watched his handiwork as the panel's golden light shimmered into existence… then slid upward. His heart sank as Count Tiberius leaped inside, clearing the book tower with pretentious grace and walking straight towards Nevian, to rub against his legs before he continued to the desk. Nevian stared at the huge cat as he once more executed a few victorious circles and settled down on his tome.

"You're the worst," he declared.

He'd wasted enough time on this. Nevian pulled his tome out from under Count Tiberius, ceded the desk to him, and plopped down on his bed with it. Unfortunately, Count Tiberius stood once robbed of his chosen seat and followed him there. He climbed on Nevian and the book at the first opportunity, eager to regain his throne. Nevian pushed him away; Tiberius returned. Nevian gritted his teeth, but he would not give up. He could be as stubborn as any cat, so he pushed him off again. The back and forth continued, and although Nevian managed to read a sentence here and there, none of the words sank into his mind, bouncing off without meaning as he continued his battle with the cat. The longer the stalemate went on, however, the thinner his patience grew.

He could be as stubborn as any cat, but he could also be cleverer.

Nevian pushed Count Tiberius away one last time, noted down the page he'd been at, then closed the book and left it on the bed. He grabbed a second one from his desk under the attentive gaze of his invader, brought it back – and sure enough, as soon as he laid it open on the sheets, Count Tiberius moved to conquer the new space. Nevian pushed him once for good measure, but when the big cat returned, he ceded territory of this new book and returned to his original read. Head on his paws, triumphantly spread over the tome, Count Tiberius watched him. Now they both had their book, and Nevian could finally return to his studies.

At first, he could barely concentrate, his gaze forever returning to Count Tiberius, convinced that at any moment now the cat would stretch and rise, opting for the book Nevian was reading instead of the one offered to him. Time passed and he remained content to stay, a silent watcher on his warm tome, and Nevian slowly recovered his focus.

He studied the transition particle, a half-rune many transmuters used to tie the two runes representing the initial and final states of the matter they transformed – a gnarly thing that felt like a foreign language all of its own, more practical sleight of hand than concrete theory, and which escaped him entirely. He understood the concept of a tie-in, like glue between the two runes, a path for magic to follow from start to finish, but not how to create them.

The dim candlelight from the distant desk wavered, its wax stretching in long arms as it reached its end, and Nevian rubbed his eyes. How long had he been at this, cross-legged on his bed, bent over his tome as he tried to unravel its mysteries? He straightened, stretching to work out a kink in his shoulder blades, a deep yawn rising from his core.

In his moment of weakness, Count Tiberius the Third struck again.

One single graceful movement brought him atop Nevian's book and lap again, and he settled down with all his weight, stretching his legs across the bed and offering his belly. Nevian stared at it, his mind slow to comprehend, still muddied by half-runes and transmutation theories he still barely grasped. Numb, he slid his fingers through the thick fur, stroking the massive cat.

Count Tiberius made his approval known through a deep, soothing rumble. It dragged a smile out of Nevian against his better judgment. He wasn't done, not if he didn't understand, but it was late and Count Tiberius was soft under his palm. He rubbed him slowly, savouring the texture, the warmth, and the simple repeated gesture – back and forth along the outstretched body, the purring intensifying with each stroke.

On some level, Nevian was aware that Count Tiberius had waited for exhaustion to take hold of him, that any victory he might've claimed for using a decoy had been temporary, but it suddenly seemed a foolish fight. He was ready to concede. Nevian slipped the book from under Count Tiberius, placing it atop the second one, then focused both hands on the long-awaited scritches.

Thoughts of transition runes slipped away, scrubbed by Count Tiberius's constant purring and the warmth of his heavy body seeping into Nevian. The last of the candlelight flickered, then vanished, dousing any possibility of returning to his studies without first removing Count Tiberius in order to stand up. Nevian had no desire to do so. He instead lay down on his bed, drowsy, and the massive cat shifted on top of him, twisting around to remain within easy reach of Nevian's hands. He let his fingers continue the slow strokes and drifted to sleep, Count Tiberius's deep purr a unique lullaby.

Claudie Arseneault is an easily-enthused aroace writer who loves to dabble in all things creative but inevitably returns to sprawling fantasy centering platonic relationships. City of Strife is the first instalment of the City of Spires trilogy, a multi-layered political fantasy led by a large, all-queer cast. When Diel Dathirii antagonizes the imperialist enclave settled near his city, he triggers a trading war that will affect every citizen of Isandor, from his noble family to the homeless living in a Shelter at its very bottom.

Wizardly Woes and Moving Mounds

Ceril N Domace

The trouble with wizards is that once they get their big, pointy hats and those fancy staffs with crystals and appropriately themed bric-a-brac attached, they start thinking they don't owe anything to anyone. They've gone through all this education, they know hundreds of spells, and they've got the credentials to prove it. In their eyes, there's no one who can judge them apart from (a select few) wizards in similar fields.

So they go ahead with their experiments "pushing the boundaries of science and magic" and creating abominations known to no god, demon, or otherworldly force that wants to get its claws into our reality. The only ones holding them back are the ethics committees at their fancy academies who, from what I can tell, are guided only by the notion that whatever research application is in front of them should go ahead because it'll be "really cool" if it works out.

And for a while, sure, it works. At least until the

plonker that chose to research sentient flame decides to go just a step further and give fire shape and a will of its own. Then the fire hamsters get out and impregnate a volcano and suddenly we have fire elementals everywhere trying to reproduce with anything that throws off a spark. Only then does the Wizard's Guild start muttering how they were "warned they were going too far" and how "lives are at stake", but the wizards can't be bothered to come down from their ivory towers to help with the situations they created. No, no, no, that would mean getting their hands dirty with the cleanup and potentially searing the bottoms of their pretentious robes and they don't have the time for that. They'll need to hire someone from outside their pristine colleges.

That's where we come in.

"We" being "Professor Clarkfowler's Exterminators, Wranglers, and Traveling Librarians", the only magical pest control company and book lender in the fifteen kingdoms. We've handled everything from brokering treaties with the sentient plant people that took over a Crosthaven noble's orchard to corralling the feral winged horses that were the brainchild of a wizard who wanted to combine the speed and flight of her favorite falcon with the durability of her witch husband's favorite mare.

Her words there, by the way, not mine. Apparently, he took it in the spirit it was intended and they're still happily married. They sent the main office a fruit basket on their anniversary from what I heard. The winged horses, in turn, became a staple export of that region.

But anyway, don't let the name fool you. I'm convinced that Professor Clarkfowler has never been nearer a place of higher learning than the front gates, if even that. Sure, she has enough books to make a wizard propose on the spot (which has happened, and more than once) and she makes all our employers pay half our bill with whatever research they have on the creatures we were hired to deal with, but she's never been to school. The most formal education she's ever undergone was the other urchins teaching her how to swear when she was little.

Allegedly, she's a full-blood human, but the pointed ears, green hair that moves against the wind, and the fact she hasn't aged a day since we met makes me highly doubt that. Not that I particularly care if someone isn't human. I'm only half myself, but at least I have the intelligence to hide my ears when I'm trying to go incognito.

I've been with her since the beginning. Back then, it was just the three of us (may the gods bless Mordecai's soul and may the various hells take the six-headed bandit that killed him) and a self-propelled wagon filled with books. It hadn't been my first choice for employment, but Professor Clarkfowler had promised me pay, beer, and a chance to get out of town fast.

Which brings us back to today, where the wagon still follows us around but now it's linked to some sort of interdimensional space Clarkfowler turned into the world's most portable library, we have nearly a hundred teams traveling from one magical monster incident to the next, and I haven't gotten a pay raise in nearly a decade. And yet somehow, I'm still the one filling out the incident reports at the end of the day. The start of the day too, come to think of it.

Take the moving mound file, for example. There were nine people present at that event, yet mine is the only report inside.

"Absolutely not. No. I refuse."

"But Garrett, think of the notes! No one's managed to find one of Klathizar's moving mounds in nearly three decades!" The professor herself pouted at me from her spot on the wagon's front seat. I wasn't allowed up there after an unfortunate incident with a flame spell gone horribly wrong, so I rode beside her on a giant stag.

He didn't have a name yet, but over the years I've found it's better to wait and see if magically modified creatures introduce themselves before I make any rash claims of ownership. I'd liberated him a few weeks back from a witch who'd thought she could short us by lying about what exactly we'd been hired to eradicate. There was a notable difference between western bog beetles and Selven's pillbugs – even a child could tell the difference between those tracks.

"He promised me a whole shelf of his bio-alchemy notes if we pinned it down," she whined, pulling her wide-brimmed hat down by the sides. "And all the big ones got killed by knights ages ago."

I snorted and vigorously shook my head. "No. Those things nearly killed us the first time we ran into them. Besides, do you even know what kind of mound this is supposed to be?"

She released her hat and flopped back into her seat. "Mostly earth, or so the rumors say," she trilled out, her pointy ears wriggling out from the mass of hair that escaped the confines of her hat. "Six farmers woke up last week and found their fields were covered in mud. They all noted a boggy odor in the air and one said she saw something bigger than a house walking off into the sunrise." She hummed for a moment and then her eyes snapped open. "You know, I bet it'd be a snap. An earthy mound has *got* to be running out of juice by now."

"You said that about the gemstone spiders and yet I'm still pulling emeralds out of the old employee records," I reminded her dryly. I paused for a moment and then added. "That was three years ago, just in case you forgot."

"They only infested the library for a few days and the carapaces sold for quite a lot of money, you have to admit," she shot back, wagging her fingers like that made up for me losing an entire set of plate mail to their appetites.

I grunted and spurred my stag forward. He chittered at me like a squirrel and I responded in kind. I wasn't sure what the witch had done to him, but he seemed to appreciate the communication attempts. Or at the very least, he fought less during bath time if I mimicked his noises while I worked.

"We're doing it and you know it," Clarkfowler said in a sing-songy tone. "It's still my company since *you* refused the management position."

I grumbled, but couldn't argue the point.

I'd refused to take her place when she wanted to retire, but I had good reason. I'd joined up with this company to get out of one position of responsibility. I wasn't looking to take on another one now, no matter how many undesirable fights it would get me out of.

"Excellent," Clarkfowler crowed, clapping to get the wagon's attention. "Wagon, alert the main office that we'll need at least six people to subdue this thing and that they should send whichever team is closest to meet us in Earden's Fallow."

I revisited my thoughts about management positions when we actually caught up to the mound. It turns out the farmers were wrong. It wasn't an earth mound. It wasn't even a mud mound. It was an entire bloody swamp.

I have no idea how Klathizar had given sentience to an entire swamp, but when I saw him next I was going to punt him from the top of his own tower. No judge in any plane of existence would blame me for killing the head of the Wizard's Guild – and most would likely shake my hand for doing so. Hang mortal laws, that man regularly violated rules of nature, celestial and demonic alike. One of those violations had just dumped me into a pond of tepid water that was more mud and rotting vegetation than liquid.

In hindsight, I should've trusted the maps. They all clearly showed that there was supposed to be a bunch of empty fields between us and Earden's Fallow, but

Drethelzam's Naiads and Queltkep's Dryads had just finished up a month-long territory battle in this area. The team we'd met up with had handled the negotiations, for crying out loud. A mile-long swamp where there used to be nothing was par for the course in situations like that.

It all would've been fine, except apparently the swamp was ticklish. The second the wagon had trundled on board, it shimmied away from the wheels, and that was how I found myself soaking wet and thinking about the course of my life.

I gave myself a few moments to ruminate and then pulled myself from the pond. Mud, muck, and rotten greenery covered every inch of me. Clarkfowler owed me for my cleaning bill and I was going to wring every last silver from her. I wasn't even going to think about the filth coating my hair right now.

It was nearly all for naught as the mound moved again, rearing up on… something. Probably legs, but I couldn't see any from this angle, so I couldn't say for sure. I grabbed onto a protruding tree, resolved firmly not to think about what body part it could correlate to, and tried to get my bearings.

At the very least, the mound wasn't moving very fast. Clarkfowler had been right about it running low on energy. Of course, that didn't make tons of earth and water falling on you any more survivable, so those who hadn't been tossed deeper in would need to be careful.

"Garrett, are you all right?" Clarkfowler's voice erupted from my pocket. "I can't see you."

If I'd been less irritated, I'd have been touched by

how concerned she sounded. As it was, I was covered in unmentionable things and soaking wet. Looping an arm around a tree for balance, I pulled my communication stone from my pocket. "I'm fine," I informed her dryly. "I'm on top of the mound. Where are you?"

"Still down on the ground, chasing after the mound. Try not to die, will you?"

I snorted in lieu of answering.

Carefully, I made my way toward a ledge in the general direction I'd come from. We'd been close to the edge when the mound woke up, so I couldn't be far away.

The shouts of the rest of our party, a mixed group of dwarves, humans, and two particularly foolhardy halflings, grew louder as I approached the ledge. The whistle of arrows and enraged shouts echoed through the pines and spruce trees. I made a mental note to review our hazard pay policy. Most of that group had been on foot and the halflings' dogs didn't run fast enough to haul them out of the way of an errant boulder should it come to that.

Actually getting to the ledge only confirmed my fears. Far below me, Clarkfowler's wagon struggled through the torn-up earth and mud. The others looked as small as cats and I swore violently.

"Language!" Clarkfowler cheerfully shouted, her voice crackling through the stone. The mound's natural magic must be interfering with our connection. "Moments of scientific discovery are no cause for vulgarity."

"Scientific discovery is going to get us killed," I shot back. I turned around and loosened my axe from its ties. "Any idea how to take this thing down?" We hadn't expected to run into the mound yet so we hadn't begun to discuss strategy beyond the standing order to do our best to survive.

We'd encountered them before, but that was decades ago. The Wizard's Guild had actually been concerned enough about the mounds to order their graduate students to help hunt them. They'd done all the heavy lifting, while we'd done our best to stay alive and distract the mounds.

Clarkfowler hummed and her voice through the stone took on an echoing bent. She must've moved to the library. "Klathizar's notes say he "imbued the heart with life and will," so I'd wager there's some sort of magic signature we should go for. If we can crack the heart without destroying it, the mound should calm down enough for us to lead it back to Klathizar's keep."

Right. Very helpful, as wizards' notes tended to be. "Anything more specific? Or should I just take a swing at anything that looks hearty?" The mound dodged left and I cursed loudly when it nearly knocked me from my perch.

She snorted. "Hardly. Knowing Klathizar it's probably something flashy near the center of the swamp. We'll try to keep it distracted from down here. Let me know if you need anything. I probably won't be able to help."

Of course not. I sighed and shoved the communication stone deep into my pocket. Pulling my axe free, I turned to the center of the mound. Time to play the part of the world's largest flea, find whatever the heart was, and hopefully not die horribly doing so.

It took hours to trek to the center of the swamp. Clarkfowler would sometimes cheerfully give updates about the battle outside but had no more luck getting someone else up here than I did finding the heart in a timely manner. My progress was continually thwarted by the swamp itself. The bog wasn't deep but it smelled worse than my stag on a hot afternoon. Plus, every root and rock I encountered was determined to knock me into every puddle and mud pit I passed.

The heart was located more or less in the center of the swamp and, like Clarkfowler predicted, it couldn't have been more clearly the heart if Klathizar had labeled it with rainbows, gemstones, and ten-foot-tall burning letters. The downside was I wasn't sure I could reach it without stepping into something that might kill me. Klathizar, unfortunately, never cut corners in his work and this was no exception.

What's more, it wasn't the swamp he had brought to life. It was the mushroom that infested and grew through the entire swamp like some fungal nervous system. That mushroom, in turn, really didn't want to die, which is why it had spent the last few decades running away from any small two-legged creatures that approached it. We weren't trying to hurt it, but it didn't know that. It just knew that people like us had killed everything like it.

The mushrooms themselves – each at least a head

taller than me – took life from a nearby spring, which I assumed was the actual heart. A gentle trickle of water flowed into and over the edges of an ancient stone bowl placed below the stream. I didn't recognize the runes covering it, but I didn't need to understand them to know that they were probably what turned the crystal-clear water pouring into the bowl to the blood pouring out.

The mushrooms all turned to face me as I approached. It's difficult to truly describe the sense of malevolence that overcame me when those fungal bastards turned my way. For one, they didn't even have faces, so I wasn't certain why they'd bothered moving at all, but I knew without a doubt that they would kill me in some horrible mushroom way if I tried to get any closer to the spring.

Sighing deeply, I pulled out my communication stone without taking my other hand off my axe. I wasn't sure what they were capable of, but I wasn't about to risk being caught off guard. "Professor, I found the heart. Any suggestions?"

It took a bit for Clarkfowler to answer and when she did she sounded tremendously out of breath. I didn't feel sorry for her at all. "You did? Excellent. The halflings keep trying to convince me we should try tripping it up, but I think Klathizar would be upset if we killed it…"

She kept speaking but I didn't pay attention to a word of it, because at that moment a mushroom-covered corpse dressed in armor with the crest of a long-gone kingdom embedded on the chest emerged from the deepest part of the spring. It held a piece of fabric that used to be white above its head like a peace flag.

I didn't attack. Mostly because it felt rude to take my axe to someone actively surrendering, no matter their present state of life or unlife, but also because the mound came to a stop once the corpse stood up.

The corpse paused at the edge of the mushrooms, where the blood leaking from the bowl turned back to water. Thin white roots connected its feet to the ground, which never quite lifted all the way up.

"Not... not hurt," it groaned out, shaking the flag like that would make its voice louder. "Talk."

I considered that statement very carefully. Intelligent undead were few and far between, but this wasn't my first encounter with sentient fungi. If they weren't given human form, many made do with what they had. There was a reason our diplomatic corps had an exceptionally fluid definition of both intelligence and what was acceptable to discuss over dinner. I should just be grateful this thing hadn't tried to implant itself in me to talk.

Sheathing my axe, I stepped forward to meet it, careful to stay out of the blood. "Professor, the mound can talk. Pull the others back, will you?"

It was company policy to accept all attempts at negotiation. An intelligent monster was one that could be persuaded to keep its rampages away from the peasantry and important trade routes. In time, many monsters became important figures in local government and trade. I'm sure this would be no different, provided it could find a fresher corpse to speak through.

The corpse nodded and its lips pulled back into something that could've been a smile.

I smiled back politely. "All right, the others should have stopped attacking you now. What can I do to resolve this situation in the way that best satisfies everyone?"

There was a reason Clarkfowler had me act as the face of the company and it wasn't just because of my good looks. I'd politicked my way through treaties between hereditary enemies, building temples for magical creatures who wanted their creators recognized as deities, and once convincing a lake of water elementals to water crops in exchange for the local fishing rights. I could handle this.

In the end, the only thing the mound wanted was someplace peaceful to put down literal and metaphorical roots. It had been running for decades now and its heart was tired. As it turned out, it was difficult for a walking swamp to settle down when most of the land in the area belonged to some lord or other that inevitably brought a wizard to find out why their most fertile farmland was practically unusable.

Fortunately, Klathizar wanted something similar, or so he said through Clarkfowler's scrying mirror, and Clarkfowler relayed to me through the stones. In his old age, he regretted the rash actions of his youth and depriving the area around his keep of all topography ranked high on that list. I figured he was just sick of seeing an empty plain when he looked outside his window, but the mound seemed pleased at the idea of returning home again so I didn't mention it.

I was happy to push the reunion, if only because we'd been promised double our standard fee if we got the mound back safely and that might just pay for the home office expansion I'd been pushing Clarkfowler to get.

The mound gently dropped me off on the ground, where Clarkfowler and the other team met me with my stag, a fresh change of clothes, and directions to a nearby stream. It shook with what I assumed to be excitement once I was safely on the ground. Mushrooms had sprouted from every bush, tree, and sufficiently-buried rock.

Clarkfowler was kind enough to park the wagon between me and the rest of the group while I scrubbed off and one of the halflings produced a lovely floral soap for my hair. I emerged a slightly cleaner, albeit chilled, man. I hung my clothes to dry on my stag's horns and my armor from the wagon's roof, remounted, and we set off for Klathizar's Keep, swamp in tow.

As we rode, the halflings entertained the party with rather dramatic descriptions of what the fight had been like from their perspective. Or at least, I hoped they were just dramatic, but Clarkfowler's periodic comments made me think they were just being honest. Our hazard payments for this quarter were going to be much higher than we budgeted for.

I let my mind wander as I rode, checking off tasks and calculating how much I could add to the bill. Klathizar would find that recovering his mound wouldn't come cheap.

I swear, if my brother and his counselors ever found me and successfully got me on that gods-forsaken throne, then every wizard in the kingdom of Hearthbreeze would have to do a semester with the pest control squads before they could graduate. I was sick and tired of this nonsense.

Ceril N Domace is an accountant, writer, and owner of a particularly feisty feline that probably wasn't the result of magical experimentation. Haven is the first book in the Fae Queen's Court series.

The Wizard's Journey

Jay Galic

The Grand Wizard of Aeon had come down from the mountain. An eternity had passed since her last descent, and those loyal acolytes who had rested at the foot of her peak to await her return had long since perished. In place of them sat their descendants. They were meek and pious, having been brought up for generations in seclusion and solitude. Their sole purpose was to devote themselves to the Wizard, and each one of them prayed that they would be fortunate enough to witness the dawn of her newest pilgrimage. When she appeared before them that morning, hovering several meters above the ground with her great silver cloak flowing in the wind, the descendants could only weep as they realised that the time of dreams was almost upon them.

They showered the Wizard with gifts as she glided through their village. Gold, holy idols and symbols, wooden effigies in her image, and the finest of silks and spices fell at her feet. She heeded none of them, refusing to speak as she passed, and showed no interest in accepting their offerings. This curtness only delighted her devotees even more. Their gratitude and love for her was never dependent on recognition or acknowledgment; her greatness was ingrained in their minds as a constant state of reality. She was their gift from some higher power, and they worshiped her freely and fearfully, in the hopes that she would grant them the one thing they had left to ask. Their dreams.

As she exited the village and disappeared into the mists below, the acolytes could only watch through their thankful tears, and pray that she would show them mercy once she reached her destination.

In truth, this was not the same Grand Wizard that their ancestors would remember, she having passed her torch onto a new heir. To insinuate that such a thing could happen would be considered blasphemy by the acolytes, but then, these men and women of faith had never been able to grasp the true nature of their object of worship.

They mattered little to the new Grand Wizard anyway, and she felt a wave of relief come over her when their village disappeared into the mist behind her.

Her journey, demanding though it was, was also quite peaceful in its solitude. Crossing through the misty hills and the barren tundra of ash and charcoal, the abandoned hamlets and the mossy cathedral ruins, the Grand Wizard hurried through the kingdom at a leisurely pace. The days grew into weeks and the weeks grew into months, and in all that time did not one situation arise where the Wizard needed to utilize her magic for defence, much to her surprise. She found her path relatively unobstructed, never running into bandits or ferocious forest beasts.

Some nights, as she used her magic to float high into the sky to sleep, she could hear the perturbed hums and clawing of the forest beasts emanating up from the darkness below her, but they were always gone come morning. A path of toppled trees and the discarded scraps of some unfortunate animal always lined the ground when the Grand Wizard descended with first light. This sight always gave the Wizard pause, unable to look away from the carnage until the sound of her heavy heartbeat became unbearable to stand. She would move more slowly on those mornings, being extra careful to look around every tree or dirt hill she passed, wrist at the ready to flick on a defensive spell should the need arise. It never did.

In addition to her defensive spells, she had been trained in using her magic to suppress her hunger for as long as her journey would take. Even so, the Grand Wizard of Aeon often found herself stopping at various villages in order to eat a good meal and to waste time.

They were built to last, thc villages. Gigantic fences made out of thick wooden stakes lined the inner sides of deep trenches. These trenches were filled with tar, mud, and the corpses of anyone unlucky enough to fall in. They only ever had one entrance, a section of the wall that could fold over by cranking a wheel on the other side, serving as a drawbridge across the trenches.

At first, the Grand Wizard would approach these villages head on, making herself known to the sentries peeking through the slits in the wooden walls.

"I am the Grand Wizard of Aeon!" she would say in

as demanding yet mystical a tone as she could muster, just like she had practiced in her head. “Let me in so I may bless your village with good fortune.” It was easy to get people to do what you wanted by offering them divine protection, so while a few villages were sceptical and apprehensive to let in a peculiar stranger who was floating several centimetres off of the ground, most dropped their gates with wide-eyed vigour, welcoming her into their homely settlements.

She was a significant distance from her mountain when she first decided to visit a village, and therefore a significant distance away from the fanatical acclamation of her acolytes. The people in these villages weren’t obsessed with her greatness, but rather treated her with awe-filled curiosity, as if she were some mythical creature they had only heard legends of. That was accurate, she supposed. Everyone knew of the Grand Wizard of Aeon, but nobody expected she would appear before them in their lifetime. It was as rare an occurrence as the moon sprouting wings and flying away, something an old myth said happens once every six thousand years. But the Grand Wizard was there because she was hungry, and she couldn’t let the upkeep of old sayings keep her from filling her stomach.

As she glided around these villages, and more people began to realize who she was, sometimes crowds would form and a cheer would commence. Enthusiastic individuals would often step forward from these crowds in attempts to strike up a chat.

“We’re all counting on you!” they would say.

"Oh, OK," she would reply nervously, without looking them in the eye. She treated conversations like her coursework back on the mountain, something she would do if necessary, but something to avoid at all cost if she had the choice. Most people caught on rather quickly and let her go about her day or finish her soup in peace. Every so often though, she would get approached by what she could only describe as packs of egotistical buffoons. Naysayers confident in their misunderstandings, who would berate her for impersonating the Wizard and demand she tell them who she really was. They were quickly shut up by a quick flick of her hand, as she used her magic to create sparks from her fingertips, or caused a small butterfly weed to sprout from her palm. Simple spells, but enough to win the Grand Wizard back her peace.

She never stayed in villages overnight, preferring instead to sleep in solitude up in the sky. Many villages pleaded with her, and attempted to get her to stay and protect their village from the horrors that lurked in the wilderness outside their walls.

"I can't forget my mission," she said on more than one occasion.

Part of her wanted to help them, to drop everything and spend a few months as protector of a village. Yet a larger part of her knew that the best way to help them would be to finish her journey and reach her destination. People kept pestering her with desperate cries for aid regardless, and it got to the point where the Grand Wizard started to sneak into villages undetected, rather than announce herself.

She would float up and over the tall fences, being extra careful not to snag her flowing silver cloak on top of one of the wooden spikes. Then, making sure that no one saw her enter the camp, she would simply find the nearest lunch line and join it. Food was scarce across the kingdom these days, and without the credibility points she gained from flaunting her title as the Grand Wizard of Aeon, some villages outright refused to feed a stranger. At other villages she was met with confused stares, but they generally let her be, and the food was hers. This way was mostly hassle-free, and she didn't have to exhaust herself with comforting rhetoric or with pretending to care for their cheers and excitement.

This worked for a while, but eventually the Grand Wizard stopped entering villages entirely. Her growing sense of uncomfortable guilt overcame her desire to eat. The Grand Wizard was supposed to be on her way to save humanity, yet instead she essentially found herself on a soup tour of the kingdom, stealing precious rations from the people she was supposed to be protecting. The Grand Wizard chided herself for her selfishness, and convinced herself she was a horrible person for putting her own wants in front of the needs of the kingdom. When feelings such as these overcame her, she would float high into the sky, away from prying eyes in order to cry. Even after she continued on her way through the kingdom, crossing dead forests and desolate wastelands, the Grand Wizard found her mind constantly drifting back to these thoughts, as well as to her doubts about the task ahead of her. She knew her goal, and she knew what was expected of her. Her teacher, the former Grand Wizard of Aeon, had taken great pains back up on the mountain to prepare her for this moment.

"You are a vessel for hope," her teacher would say as she glided around, her lifeless silver eyes peering down over the trembling form of her apprentice. "This is your purpose for being. You will not fail. Do you understand?"

The Grand Wizard knew this truth, had lived it her whole life, yet she was terrified nonetheless. If she failed her task and ruined the kingdom's final chance at a better future, the Grand Wizard was certain she would not be able to recover from the thousands of disappointed faces being cast her way. These thoughts, amongst a slew of others, constantly swirled around inside her as if a dust devil had been let loose in her mind, tearing her brain to pieces. But these were not thoughts that a Grand Wizard of Aeon should have, and so she cast them to the back of her mind as often as she could.

Then at long last, after twelve full moons, the Grand Wizard's pilgrimage came to its end as she arrived at the stone gate in the cliff-side by the Sea of Remembrance. The sea, radiant in its goldenrod hue, sparkled in the late afternoon sun. Its beauty extended out over the horizon for as far as she could see, tempting the Grand Wizard to stay by its shores an extra night. She lay there in the dusty sands, looking out into the night sky and taking in the cascading sounds of the waves against the beach.

This was her last chance to breathe before her destiny. Her final night of rest.

The Grand Wizard of Aeon hadn't had a single dream since leaving her mountain home a year ago, yet on that night, where she decided to sleep next to the golden waters of the sea, her sleep was filled with an assortment of images and colours, mesmerizing shapes and hues crashing and merging into one another in a beautiful dance. At first they made little sense, but soon the shapes and colours began to coalesce into more concrete images. They formed a manifestation of herself as a young girl, watching as her parents left her with the bishops, a wide smile on Father's face and a bag full of gold over Mother's shoulder.

"You have a duty," the bishops said in unison as they walked her into the cathedral. "You will save the world."

She then saw herself as someone she didn't recognize, older and bursting with confidence – a form she felt would never come to pass. She stood atop a massive waterfall that towered over the sun, spilling silver liquid out into the cosmos of space. She was being swept up by the current and quickly getting sent towards the edge. She tried to fight it, to swim against the push, but to no avail. As she scrambled to live she was cast over the side, falling with the silver liquid into the vast unknown, and her soul was lost forever.

The Grand Wizard awoke with a start.

She still lay on the beach, shivering and sweating, using her silver cloak as a blanket. It was dangerous to sleep so exposed, as the forest beasts – or who knew what else – could appear from any shadow. The Grand Wizard found she didn't care. She curled up, pulling her legs to her chest and closing her eyes tight. She didn't try to sleep, she only cried and hoped to forget everything for once. She pretended she was on a holiday with her parents to some exotic beach resort. A book she had read on the mountain had mentioned such a thing. She remembered reading it, fully engrossed, waiting for the day her parents would return for her and take her there with them. They never came, but the thought helped her relax for a small moment.

In the morning, when the sun was well and truly residing over the land, the Grand Wizard arose and used her magic to blow a gust of wind over her body to shake off all of the sand. Then with a flick of her hand, she opened the large stone gate in the cliff side by the water and floated down into the place of the kingdom's dreams.

This was the Cavern of Fantasy, and the Grand Wizard thought it dull. She found herself atop a spiral stairwell that sank deep into the ground. The walls were made of dirt, with roots and various unknown minerals interspersed throughout. It looked just like a standard cave, and certainly didn't resemble the breathtaking majesty she had been expecting. As she floated deeper down the stairs, however, the brown dullness of the cavern walls began to shift, and the Grand Wizard caught herself gasping in amazement. In place of the craggy soil, the walls now displayed an assortment of fantastical colours. Reds and greens, blues and yellows, all spinning around her and covering the cavern in a spectacular shine of shimmering light. It was as if she had somehow stumbled inside of her kaleidoscope, her favourite childhood toy. The Grand Wizard recalled her dream from the previous night, and how similar it had looked to what she was experiencing now. *Perhaps the Cavern was calling out to me,* she thought, *begging me to enter and complete my destiny.*

As she continued further, the Grand Wizard was so entranced by the beauty of the colours around her that she almost missed an opening carved into the side of the wall. She had to look hard to distinguish it, as the colours glided over it as if it were just another section of the wall, hiding it from all but the most astute. Any untrained eye that somehow managed to bypass the stone gate and enter the Cavern of Fantasy by mistake would be too enamoured by the colours to see it, continuing down the staircase in a never-ending spiral for all of eternity. A magical defence that the cavern created to protect itself from the unworthy, her teacher had warned her.

She floated towards the opening, passing through the stream of colours and entering a large dome-shaped room. This room retained the psychedelic colour palette of the stairwell, and the Grand Wizard noted how impossibly smooth the walls and ceiling looked, causing an eerie shiver to descend down her spine. The room was completely bare, save for a small fissure filled with liquid at the centre of the cave.

This was the Pool. It was crusty at the edges and uneven in its dimensions, putting it at odds with the uniform neatness of the room's design. It was filled to the brim with a thick silvery liquid that looked not unlike mercury. The Grand Wizard knew it wasn't of course, although neither she – nor her predecessors – knew what it really was. They only knew what it did.

The Grand Wizard glided across the room, coming to a rest by the edge of the Pool and letting her exposed feet touch the ground for the first time since entering the Cavern of Fantasy. The simple act of making physical contact with the floor caused an intense rush of magical energy to flow through her body. The Grand Wizard had been trained to withstand such an onrush of magic power, but the sheer amount of it encroaching inside her body all at once was almost enough to make her lose balance. She held fast, calling upon all of her training, all of her knowledge of magic and the magical world, and after a minute had passed, she found that she had successfully acclimated to the force of the room and was able to carry on with the task at hand.

Kneeling down in front of the Pool, the Grand Wizard removed the white hood of her cloak, and looked down into the silvery liquid. On its surface she saw the reflection of a face. It had light brown hair flowing down beneath the shoulders, and green eyes that seemed to be faded over, lost in something resembling thought, but with no clear direction. It was the reflection of a face that might have once belonged to a single young woman, but was now the property of the kingdom she served. It was a face resigned to a purpose, one she mustn't fail at. The Grand Wizard took a deep breath, and slowly lowered her face toward the Pool, breaking the surface and sinking her head deep into the silver liquid of dreams.

She held her breath for a few moments, steeling herself and casting out any last-minute doubts. Finally, knowing there was nothing else to do before the end, she opened her mouth, letting the silver liquid invade her body and enter her lungs. It wasn't as painful as she thought it would be – in fact, she felt almost soothed, as if she were diving into the warm waters of an herbal spa. She almost couldn't tell she was drowning.

Opening her eyes, she saw the dreams of the kingdom laid out in front of her, taking form as several mist-like clouds dispersed throughout the wistful waves of the silver liquid. There were thousands of them, maybe millions. Each one displayed an image, an idea, a hope that had been wished by someone in the not-too-distant past. Kings and queens, peasants and merchants, the faithful and the faithless alike – each one had a dream that they wished to be fulfilled. The Pool was the conduit of these dreams, a library that collected all of them in place to await the arrival of the Grand Wizard of Aeon. This was what her life had been building up to; choosing whose dreams she would grant, and whose she would forsake.

She saw all kinds of dreams. Some were simple and personal, such as a lonely old farmer wishing for his long-deceased love to be brought back into his arms. Others concerned the world as a whole, like the young prince who longed for true peace and stability in his kingdom. Dream after dream flooded her senses, each one reaching out toward her, calling her, begging her to choose them and make them a reality.

As the silvery liquid filled her, her magical powers were amplified to a point that nobody except previous Grand Wizards could ever understand. It gave her the power to grant these wishes, as many as she desired, for as long as she stayed conscious. And although she would die due to this process, it was a sacrifice she had been prepared for. It was her destiny, after all.

After the deed was done, and the dreams of the kingdom had been realised, the silver liquid would consume her, enchanting her body and taking it over as its new vessel. Her soul would be dead, and her body would be nothing more than a mist-like wraith, kept moving by some higher force of nature. It would be sent back up the mountain, ready to train and prepare the next Grand Wizard for their own self-sacrificing crusade.

The Grand Wizard remembered when her teacher had first announced what was going to happen to her once she arrived at the Cavern of Fantasy. They had been in the middle of an early morning lesson in one of the lesser gardens of the mountain. Her teacher had said it so quickly and easily that the Grand Wizard was certain she had misheard. She hadn't, and her teacher's emotionless stare – eyes stained with silver – proved it. She had cried that night when she was certain her teacher couldn't hear. Her mind, her heart, her soul: everything that made her who she was would be snuffed out eternally. Since that day, she believed she had made peace with the fact, truly understanding her sacrifice was necessary to beget a new and prosperous era for the kingdom. Still, feelings of dread and uncertainty had plagued her mind in the years building up to her arrival at the Pool. To be able to willingly face certain death without a single doubt or fear in mind... People are rarely that stoic.

Time was running short. She could feel the silver's hold on her body getting stronger. The Grand Wizard attempted to ignore her grating fear as best she could, and focus her remaining strength on choosing a dream to make real. She wanted to choose a grand dream that benefited all, one that would be worth her death. She began sifting through the clouds again, searching for something, anything, she deemed worthy, and she found many that were. Dreams from hopeful people in hopeless situations. But while the Grand Wizard saw their hopes and felt their pain in a more intimate way than they themselves could ever know, it didn't take long before she stopped searching for dreams altogether. Instead she simply floated in the silver, motionless, listening to the silence.

In one swift motion, she ripped her head out of the Pool, splashing droplets of the sacred silver liquid onto the cavern floor. Coughing and gasping for air, it took her several minutes to regain her natural senses, having become so used to the whims of the silver. She sat there for a moment that lasted forever, her head dripping liquid magic, blankly staring at the Pool's surface.

Her mind was a mess, desperately trying to justify her actions. The kingdom had been ravaged by decades of war and years of neglect. Drought and famine were all the current generation knew, and the only thing keeping them going was the distant hope that the fabled Grand Wizard of Aeon would descend from her mountain and save them from their pain. She knew she needed to do it. She knew she had to do it. Yet despite knowing this fact in the deepest crevice of her heart, the Grand Wizard could not bring herself to re-enter the Pool. She could not bring herself to make even one dream a reality. She could not bring herself to die.

And then, as if the state of her mind was a signal to the world itself, the Cavern of Fantasy began to react. The cave began to tremble, and the colours on the walls rapidly changed in violent flashes. The Grand Wizard, having snapped out of her daze, began to panic. She looked down at the Pool and let out a cry as she saw the silver liquid begin to move. No longer smooth and docile, the liquid was now writhing, forming waves and crashing into itself. Pulsating and bubbling, the liquid lapped over the edges of the Pool like a dish of boiled water.

As the Grand Wizard watched, the liquid suddenly lurched and reached out towards her, causing her to fall back. As if it had come alive, the liquid began to rise, overflowing the pool. It slid along the polished ground, slowly moving towards the flustered Grand Wizard. She couldn't comprehend what she was seeing, and crawled backwards to escape, never taking her eyes off of the encroaching slime. When she felt her back hit the wall of the cavern, she instinctively raised her hand and fired a spark of electricity at the liquid as it approached. Her bolt hit, but seemed to have no effect. The liquid was spread out wide across the floor, a thin film of bubbling silver slowly moving to cover more and more of the ground.

The Grand Wizard's mind raced to remember some of the defensive techniques she had learned in her training. She hadn't used many of them in over a year, and couldn't quite recall the signs she would have to mime in order to cast them. She cursed herself for not practicing her magic more on her journey. She looked around in desperation, searching for the door she had come in by, but couldn't find it anywhere. Had it disappeared or was it simply hidden by the colours again? She couldn't say, but the Grand Wizard knew that the panic she felt in her heart would prevent her from focusing enough to find it. Trembling, she glanced over at the silver and let out a gasp at what she saw.

It had stopped its advance. Instead, it had started to writhe once more, stretching out and crashing into itself, forming incoherent and grotesque shapes. Its violent pulsation gave the impression that it was in agony, that it was struggling to overcome something. Then the liquid began to shimmer, and in a flash of blinding white light, all of it disappeared.

In that single moment, the Grand Wizard felt an intense and sharp pain flow through her body. The magical energy in the cave had suddenly vanished, giving her whiplash and causing her to retch. The rainbow walls around her had changed to a monotone grey, which then dissipated completely, revealing the cave as the grubby dirt-filled burrow it truly was. Finally, the cavern's trembling ceased, leaving the room still and silent.

The Grand Wizard sat in shock, breathing heavily. She sat for a while, waiting to see if anything else would happen, but nothing did. The room looked so completely different that it almost seemed like another place entirely.

The Grand Wizard stood up, and began to walk slowly towards the middle of the room. The floor she stood on was no longer smooth, and some of the sharper rocks that jutted out of the ground dug into her exposed feet, drawing blood. She hardly noticed, and continued walking until she was standing over a small hole in the ground at the centre of the cave. This had once been the Pool, but now it looked like nothing more than a misshapen trench haphazardly dug into the dirt. The Grand Wizard couldn't feel any traces of magical energy, and tears began to fall from her eyes.

The Pool was dry, and the Grand Wizard of Aeon could no longer complete her destiny. She could only stare in disbelief. She waited for the Pool to fill up again, in a naive hope that it'd simply refill over time. But she knew that would never happen, and she raised her hands to her crying face, slowly crouching down on the floor.

All she felt was shame, a deep shame that made her sick to her stomach. No wish would be granted on this day, or any day in the future. She didn't quite understand what had happened, but what she had felt when the liquid disappeared had had a sense of finality to it, as if a loved one had died. The only thing she knew for certain was that she was to blame. By leaving the Pool when she did, she had forsaken her destiny, the kingdom and everyone in it. One brief moment of weakness, and she had killed the magic of the cave.

The Grand Wizard fell towards the shallow Pool, clawing at the dirt inside, trying to somehow bring back the liquid. *I made a mistake*, she thought, *please give me another chance and I won't falter!* She pleaded to any god or deity that would listen, searching for some way to redeem herself and put things right. Her pleas had no effect. The Grand Wizard continued to plead regardless, over and over again, and she continued to dig until her fingers were stained with dirt and blood. Eventually though, she gave up, knowing deep in her heart that nothing would bring back her destiny.

Alina hadn't moved for several hours. She sat against the wall of what once would have been called the Cavern of Fantasy, but which now seemed less impressive than a latrine pit. Winding roots pierced the damp dirt that made up the ceiling and walls. Crumbly and uneven, the whole place seemed as if it could cave in at any second. Alina's injured feet had left dark streaks of red along the sharp floor of the cavern. She should have been feeling pain, but instead she simply felt numb.

She could no longer call herself 'The Grand Wizard of Aeon', as what sort of Grand Wizard would punish the people she was charged to protect, due to her own selfish desire to live? No, Alina was sure she no longer deserved the title.

She had been twelve years old when she had set out from her mountain home about a year ago. Her thirteenth birthday must have passed somewhere along the way, although she hadn't a clue when. Alina's sole contact on the mountain, her teacher, had never thrown her a party, or wished her a happy birthday, or even acknowledged her existence outside of their lessons at all. She had never understood why her teacher had always been so cold, but she knew now with absolute clarity. It was because there was never anybody inside. Her teacher's lifeless silver eyes should have given it away, but she never thought about it in much detail until now. Her teacher was a vessel, consumed by the silver. She had never been anything else.

Alina groaned, burying her head deeper into her knees. She passed several more hours in this state, hardly moving an inch. Eventually, she could no longer ignore the stinging of the cuts on her feet. So the former Grand Wizard of Aeon finally stood up, and carefully began walking out of the dead cavern.

It was night-time now, and the solitary moon reflected beautifully in the golden sea. As she came to a rest by the entrance of the cave, she felt her body ache, and knew that that it wasn't just her feet that were injured. She glided over to a smooth stone that was protruding from the water, and, facing the beach, sat down to inspect herself. The events of the day seemed to have taken their toll on her as several bloody cuts and bruises dotted her body.

Biting her lip to try and mask the pain, she shifted so that she was sitting cross-legged, and began to mime a spell. She flicked her wrist a certain way, and her palms began to glow a faint green colour. She lowered her glowing hands to her wounds, and began the process of healing. She worked with the waves as her backdrop, and let their melodic crashing and waning soothe her soul.

And it was there, as Alina sat cross legged on a mighty stone on the beach, that a change occurred within her. It wasn't instant, but as she whiled away the hours slowly healing her broken body, Alina found that the intense swarm of emotions that had encapsulated her mind since the incident at the Pool had receded, being replaced now by another distinct feeling.

She felt calm.

Taking in a deep breath of salty sea air, Alina closed her eyes, and revelled in the meditative state she had found herself drifting into. She didn't cry. She didn't speak. She didn't think.

She simply was.

Since the end of her journey, Alina's emotions had been high and her thoughts had been a mess. They still were, to a certain extent. But as she sat there in silence, letting the wind rush over her and bathe her clean of her bitter thoughts, she couldn't help but smile.

Jay Galic works as a submissions manager for Andromeda Spaceways Magazine, has plans to launch an online serialised fiction project in the near future, and hopes to generally write a lot more.

Bad Blood

Josie Jaffrey

The bright afternoon was shading into evening as Cam headed across Solomon College's main quad. The sun was shining, the breeze was rustling and the birds were singing until, quite suddenly, they weren't. Generations of evolution had done their job well. When you roost in the halls of the world's premiere college of vampires – the Silver, they call themselves – then either you attune your senses quickly or you end up as roast pigeon. The birds' silence gave Cam enough warning to race around the corner into the science quad just in time to see the lab windows blow out, propelled by gouts of sulphuric smoke.

"Oh no, not again," he groaned.

He burst into the central laboratory to find the occupants spluttering. There were three of them, as usual, crouching behind one of the benches like naughty schoolboys.

"That was an interesting reaction," said the first. This was Dr Edmund Castell, Cam's boyfriend and scientific reprobate.

"I guess that answers the question about whether or not we have the acid ratio correct." This was the second, Dr Jahan Khalyed.

"A resounding *no*," replied the third, Dr Kayode

Ladipo.

The three doctors did not look at all similar under normal circumstances. Ed was just under six feet tall, pale-skinned and dark-haired, with a tightly-muscled frame that went unremarked under his lab coat. Dr Kay was taller still, rangy, dark-skinned, and wore his hair in close-cut curls that were usually immaculate. By contrast, Dr Jay was shorter than average, about five foot six, with mid-brown skin, unruly dark hair, a definite paunch and a permanent grin. But right now, the only thing to distinguish the three crouching forms was the fact that a small portion of Ed's face had been saved from the blast by the protection of his glasses. Every other inch of them was covered in burns, punctured by shrapnel or slick with blood. Their wounds would have killed the average human, but fortunately they each had the supernatural strength and healing ability that was part and parcel of the Silver bargain.

"You have no eyebrows," Cam said to Ed.

"Good thing I was wearing these, then," Ed replied, tapping the lens of his specs. Like all the Silver, Ed had 20/20 vision, so the glasses were pure affectation, an odd fashion statement that Cam found indecipherable yet strangely endearing. Now that Ed had proved they could be used as makeshift goggles, Cam was sure he would never hear the end of it. He eyed the three blood- and soot-covered faces with a concern they didn't seem to share.

"What happened this time?"

Ed waved a hand dismissively. "Just a small

miscalculation."

A raft of ceiling tiles crashed onto the floor between them, dragging a piece of mangled copper piping in its wake. A steady stream of water followed.

"*Small*?" Cam squeaked.

"Comparatively," Ed conceded. "At least the roof stayed on this time."

Dr Jay dusted off his lab coat, shedding chunks of plaster and glass as he got to his feet, while Dr Kay picked himself up from the debris and walked over to the doors – now hanging off their hinges – where a battered sign read *20 days since last explosion.* He rubbed out the *2*.

"Kayode!" The abused doors finally gave up and crashed into the rubble as Adinde Ladipo, Dr Kay's wife and one of Cam's fellow Seekers, pushed her way into the lab. "Are you okay?" She took Dr Kay's face in her hands, tutted with sympathy, then started pulling wooden splinters and bits of glass from his skin. "I wish you'd be more careful. It's going to take pints of blood for you to heal all this damage."

Meanwhile, Dr Jay had righted a toppled lab bench and was replacing the radio on top, which, miraculously, was still blaring out Eiffel 65's *Blue (Da Ba Dee)*.

Ed eyed the radio mournfully. "I was the hoping the explosion might have saved us from that racket."

"What are you talking about?" said Dr Jay. "It's great! So bouncy. So danceable." He shook his round backside to the beat.

"It's ludicrous," said Ed. "All modern music is

pointless rubbish."

"Pff, you think anything after the eighteenth century is modern. We have to move with the times! Surely you've spent enough centuries on this planet to know that evolution is not optional. Adapt or die, my friend."

"I think I'd rather die," Ed muttered, glaring at the radio.

"It's all a matter of perspective, you know," said Dr Jay, accepting the bottle of blood that Adinde had retrieved from the one unscathed fridge. "In its day, Pirates of Penzance was considered puerile dross too."

Dr Kay abruptly stopped drinking from his own bottle.

"Jahan," he said, stony-faced. "You can play whatever cacophony you like, but do not disparage Gilbert and Sullivan by comparing it to this… this… nonsense."

"But it's true! We must embrace change, or get left behind in its wake."

"I'd like you to embrace a change in your working methods," said Adinde. "I could do without my husband being blown up twice a month, and you're burning through the college blood supply."

"Ah." Dr Jay held up a finger. "You see, that's the whole point of this glorious new endeavour. We're developing a formula that will let the Silver body heal *without* the consumption of human blood."

"You mean you expect us to drink the stuff that just exploded all the windows?" Cam said, horrified.

"Well, obviously it needs a little refining, but when it's ready, just imagine: we'll have a world without

Silver predation. We won't need human blood anymore. It'll be a revolution! Freedom! Utopia!"

"If we can get it to work," said Dr Kay.

"And I have no doubt that we shall. Let's get back to it, shall we?" Dr Jay gathered up what he could salvage from the rubble on the floor – a singed notebook, a Bunsen burner, a single unbroken crucible – and carried it all into the lab next door as though he wasn't leaving a bomb site behind him. Dr Kay and Ed followed.

Adinde looked at her watch and sighed. "They'll be here all night again, won't they?"

"Looks like it," said Cam. He surveyed the carnage. "Good thing there are no murders for us to investigate at the moment."

"I don't know. I might contemplate causing one if there are many more lab accidents."

"They'll crack it eventually, one way or another." Cam put his arm around Adinde's shoulders and gave her a consoling squeeze. "They always do."

"Just like they always leave us to sort out the mess." She sighed again, resigned now to the inevitable. "All right. You fetch the clean up crew and I'll beg some more blood from the canteen. If they're pulling another all-nighter then they'll need their strength."

As it happened, they'd been closer to the solution than even Dr Jay had dared to hope. It was barely ten o'clock that same evening when Dr Kay finished distilling the final ingredient, poured it carefully – oh so carefully – into the flask Ed had prepared, and nodded for Dr Jay to add the catalyst powder. He did so at arm's length, cringing involuntarily away from the mixture as the other two hid out in the corridor, at Cam and Adinde's prior insistence.

All three held their breath for one, two, three seconds.

Nothing.

Gingerly, Dr Jay stirred the contents of the flask with a glass rod. It turned a slightly darker shade of red, but that was it.

No fizzing. No popping. No exploding.

"We did it," said Dr Kay. He took a series of slow, disbelieving steps back into the lab. "We really did it."

"Maybe," said Ed, following him in. "There's no way to know for sure until we test it."

"I'll test it," Dr Kay volunteered.

"Hang on, now," said Dr Jay, whose attempts to tamp down his excitement were somewhat undermined by the fact that he was grinning from ear to ear. "I know we're all feeling keen, but there's no reason to rush straight into Silver trials."

"Why not?" said Dr Kay. "The formula is hardly going to hurt us. Almost nothing does."

"I don't know," said Ed. "We're messing with the basic biochemical functions of the Silver, which – let's be honest – we don't fully understand ourselves. I think some caution would be well-advised."

"Exactly," said Dr Jay, though it looked like the restraint was costing him. "There's no call to go letting our curiosity get the better of us. We're scientists. We have to approach this rationally."

"Spoilsport," said Dr Kay.

"Child," Dr Jay replied.

"Idiots," muttered Ed.

And so the night passed in gentle bickering and experimental invention as they tried between the three of them to come up with a suitable proof for their new serum. The problem was that the Silver body was so fiendishly complicated in its workings – more complicated even than the human body – that creating a useful test environment was nigh-on impossible. So far, there was no solution, but they were all bloody-minded and highly motivated. They would not give up.

The last thing Dr Jay remembered was Ed calling it a night shortly after four a.m., then he was waking up with a crick in his neck and his cheek stuck to the bench top with drool.

"Ugh," he groaned. "Kay?" His voice sounded as rough as he felt. "Kayode?"

He blinked the sleep from his eyes and peered around the lab, surprised to find himself alone. Dr Kay usually stayed by his side until the bitter end when he worked late, too competitive to abandon the lab before Dr Jay did. Adinde must have bullied him into his bed while Dr Jay was out for the count.

He couldn't remember the last time he'd fallen asleep over his work. He must have taken more damage in the explosion than he'd realised.

Stretching his stiff muscles, he pushed back from the mess of notes spread on the bench in front of him and made his way over to the glass-fronted fridge at the back of the lab to survey the fruits of yesterday's labours. They might not have a working test for it yet, but they'd cracked the formula, he was sure. They'd really cracked it. Those two vials contained the key to… Those two vials…

He rubbed his eyes and looked again.

That *one* vial.

After they'd distilled the last of their precious components – some of which were so fiddly that they would take months to replicate – and refined their catalysts, they'd been able to make enough serum to fill just two vials. Now one of them was missing.

Only one explanation presented itself.

No.

Kayode wouldn't have tested the serum on himself, not after they'd all expressly agreed to devise some form of non-Silver testing first. Not when they had so little of the serum to spare. Not when Adinde would be so dead-set against it.

Or would he?

Then he heard the screaming.

Dr Jay raced out of the lab, following Adinde's cries to the main quad where he found Dr Kay on his back on the grass, still wearing yesterday's soot-stained and ragged clothes.

"What did you do?" she yelled. Dr Jay was already protesting his innocence when he realised that she wasn't yelling at him, but at her husband. "Why would you take such a stupid risk?" She fixed her streaming eyes on Dr Jay. "Why would you let him?"

"I was asleep," he said. "I didn't know…"

The duty doctor was seconds behind Dr Jay, rushing

from the direction of sick bay with Ed on her heels.

"My god," she said, one hand on Dr Kay's forehead, "he's boiling hot. What happened?"

"There's a vial missing from the lab," Dr Jay said. "I think he must have–"

"A vial of what?"

"It's experimental. It was supposed to stop the Silver from needing to drink blood, but…" He was too ashamed to attempt any further explanation. It was clear from the scathing look he received from the duty doctor that she already thought little enough of the idiot scientists who'd created the mess she would now have to clean up.

"There's this too," Adinde said, pulling down Dr Kay's collar. There was a darker patch across one side of his throat, as black and textured as cooled lava, about the size of a lump of coal, with a glowing spot of heat at its centre. It looked as though the serum was burning him up from the inside.

The doctor took one look and shuddered.

"Help me get him to sick bay," she said to Adinde. "Now."

From that point on, Dr Jay and Ed were superfluous. Their doctorates were in various branches of the sciences, but neither of them had studied medicine to the level required to treat the Silver. Dr Jay reflected mournfully that perhaps they should have taken that fact into consideration before attempting the formula in the first place.

"We're done," said Dr Jay, pulling Ed back as he

turned towards the lab. "It's over. No more."

"But maybe," Ed protested, "if we could just work out where it went wrong, then we could fix it and–"

"No. It's out of our hands. It never should have been in them."

"But we were so close."

"Close enough that we nearly killed Kayode."

It was a sobering thought, because Dr Kay wasn't out of the woods yet. Although experience dictated that a Silver could survive practically anything, there was still no guarantee. He might never recover from this.

"Go home," Dr Jay said. "I'll clear the lab and lock up the rest of the serum, so we can make sure this doesn't happen again. You get some rest, and tomorrow we'll start work on something new. Something safer."

With Dr Kay, he hoped.

It took some time for Dr Jay to pack away the remains of their last, ill-fated experiment. He had a locked cool box that they used to store some of their more valuable and volatile elements, which he emptied out to make room for the last vial of serum. He didn't think Ed would touch it, and Dr Kay was in no fit state to take a second dose, but just to be extra sure, Dr Jay reset the combination lock and chose a new code. Now he would be the only one with access and the only one to blame if something went wrong. That made him feel more comfortable, because shouldn't the responsibility have been his all along? It felt like his fault that his friend was hurt, and he wanted to take the weight of that burden.

He rubbed his eyes and moaned with a heady mix of

heartache and exhaustion.

What in the world could have possessed Dr Kay to do something so stupid? And how could Dr Jay have let it happen? He shouldn't have fallen asleep. He should have locked up the serum earlier. He should have done anything except let his friend put himself in such danger.

But the hard reality was that there was no changing the past. He had to focus on the present.

Finally, he packed up his notes and carried them over to sick bay to share the formula with the duty doctor. If he could help in no other way, then perhaps explaining the details of the serum's constitution and how it was *supposed* to work might help with Dr Kay's treatment.

But it didn't look good.

Although the duty doctor assured him that Dr Kay was slowly recovering, it was hard to see the evidence of that in his face or on his skin. When Dr Jay sat next to the bed and took Dr Kay's hand in his own, it was almost too hot to hold. There was sweat pouring down his friend's face and the lava-like scab remained on his neck, still as dark and blistered as ever. A day's worth of intravenous blood should have healed a surface wound like that without much trouble, but whatever was wrong clearly went beyond that.

"I've sent Adinde to get some food," said the duty doctor, "but she won't stay away for more than half an hour. If I were you, I'd be gone before she gets back."

Dr Jay nodded his thanks, accepting the advice and the warning in her tone. He could understand why

Adinde might not want to be around him right now. Truth be told, he didn't much want to be around himself either. The quiet in sick bay wasn't helping. There was nothing to listen to except the ticking of the clock, the gentle beep of the machines and the constant recriminations that crowded his head.

Kayode Ladipo was special. Ed was a relative newcomer to the college, but Dr Jay and Dr Kay went back more than a century together. From the moment the two of them had met, they'd formed a perfect double-act: Dr Jay and Dr Kay, the lab guys, each the perfect foil to the other. It's not often that you find someone so attuned to your personality, and it had happened to Dr Jay precisely once. Ed had slotted into their dynamic well, but he'd never be as close to either of them as they were to each other. They had the kind of relationship that's forged in decades of late nights and hard problems, problems so hard that you could only solve them through weeks and months of agonising calculations and exhausting experimentation. Work like that required absolute trust and absolute respect, which is exactly what Dr Jay and Dr Kay gave each other.

And in one mad night, they had thrown it all away.

Dr Kay's eyelids flickered and he moaned, a sound that was made no less anguished by its softness.

"I'm so sorry," Dr Jay whispered, squeezing his friend's hand. He watched Dr Kay's eyelids for movement, but they were still now.

"When will he wake up?" Dr Jay asked the duty doctor.

"I don't know." She was concentrating on the papers he had given her, flicking through his barely-decipherable notes. "This serum of yours has really done a number on him. I'm not sure…"

"What?"

She met his eyes. "I'm not entirely sure that he'll wake up at all."

No, Dr Jay said to himself as he strode back to the lab. *I will not accept this.*

He took a clean lab coat from the hook inside the door and shrugged it on over his ripped and filthy clothes. He shouldn't be here, he knew. He should take the good advice he had given to Ed and walk away from this, go home to sleep it off, but his heart was overruling his brain's every objection.

I made a mistake, but I can fix it. I can find a way to make him better.

A surge of optimism pulsed through him. He'd always tended towards problem-solving, and despite the gravity of the situation, he felt now the way he always felt when faced with a conundrum. Perhaps recent experiences should have tempered his enthusiasm, but despite what he had told Ed, he just knew that the solution was within his reach.

All of a sudden, he believed it implicitly. He could correct the serum and make it do what it was supposed to do in the first place, then he could give it to Dr Kay and let it fix the serum that was still burning within his body. He could fix Dr Kay.

It would work. It had to work.

The certainty came over him in a fervour, compelling him to action until he felt delirious with its effects. He'd been driven in his research before, through sleepless nights and caffeinated days, but never like this, never to the point that his hands shook with frustrated energy. When finally, after many hours, he unlocked the precious remaining vial of serum and poured it into his new concoction, he had to steady his hand at the wrist to prevent himself from spilling it all over the bench.

And then it was done.

Dr Jay knew that it was perfect. There was something about the vibrancy in the new shade of red it had turned, something in the sheen of the meniscus within the flask that told him that, this time, it was exactly what it was supposed to be.

The problem was that he couldn't just give it to Dr Kay, not after what had happened last time. He would have to test it first, but they never had managed to come up with an appropriate proof to satisfy themselves that the serum would be safe for consumption.

Which meant there was only one option.

It was madness after what had happened to Dr Kay, but…

With a quick prayer, Dr Jay picked up the flask and tipped it back in one long, smooth gulp. With it went the last trace of the first serum, but that wasn't a concern. He'd only need to administer the new additives to Dr Kay, and they were easily assembled. As for replicating the complete second serum for future use, he really couldn't have cared less. Besides, if it didn't work, then it was best that the formula be buried forever, probably along with Dr Jay. If it did, then they could always extract samples from his blood.

His blood…

His blood was *hot*. His pulse was racing, thudding in his chest in a way that he had never experienced since he turned Silver. Back when he'd been a human, maybe, but this flushing, boiling, *burning* heat was unbearable. There were dark spots pulsing in his vision, coalescing and growing every time they flashed to the rhythm of the crushing pain in his head. He tried to blink them away, but it felt as though he was closing his eyelids over broken glass, which was when the pain finally released him into blissful unconsciousness.

When Dr Jay woke in the dark, for a moment he thought he had lost his sight entirely. Then he realised he could make out the edges of the lab windows by the ambient streetlight outside. In a few blinks, his Silver vision was back and the world was just as detailed as it had ever been. With it came the rest of his senses: the taste of the serum in his throat, the sound of bats flying around the college towers, the smell… The *smell*.

The smell was incredible. It was like blood, but not quite. There was something different about it, something sweeter and richer and deeper.

He had to have it.

Without thinking at all, following only the imperatives of his body, he let his nose guide his feet out of the lab and into the college quad. The scent was everywhere, and it was intoxicating. It hung in trails in the air, winding through the spring trees and masking the scent of the daffodils so that Dr Jay could smell nothing beyond or underneath it. He was fixated. The scent was everything, the *only* thing, and his body wanted it.

There.

His head snapped around as a door opened on the other side of the quad and a man walked out into the night. He was Silver – Dr Jay could tell that by the slow thud of his heartbeat – but he didn't look familiar. He must be visiting the college, perhaps even from another country–

Irrelevant, his nose insisted. *This is what I need.*

Dr Jay, mindless, obeyed.

As he sank his teeth into the man's neck, he realised that he had been wrong. They'd all been wrong. Dr Kay hadn't drunk the first vial at all.

He had.

It was a glimpse of a memory, barely more than a dream, but he remembered this feeling. He remembered the fire in his blood, the way it demanded something that wasn't quite human. The way the desire for that thing had overwhelmed his senses, leading him by his nose to the closest source, to sink his teeth into the neck of his dearest friend.

The terrible truth was that the first serum had worked, and his adjustments had only made it more powerful. It had done exactly what they'd designed it to do: it allowed the Silver to live without drinking *human* blood. But the cost, this uncontrollable and destructive thirst, was terrible.

The fire burning in Dr Jay's veins was pouring out of him now as he quenched it with the Silver blood that spilled into his mouth and filled his body. As the blood flowed in, the fire flowed out into the stranger he'd grappled into his arms, and it *burned.* It blazed through the man's body, bursting cells and cauterising arteries as it went. He could feel the skin heating beneath his fingers until it was like boiling water, like molten glass, like the white heart of a Bunsen's flame.

There was a blaze of brightness and then there was nothing at all, just a memory of a body flaking away into ash in his hands. The man was gone, disintegrated into a pile of dust at his feet. All that remained of him was the blood filling Dr Jay's body.

His feet took him back to the lab and, in its dark embrace, he put his head down on the bench in despair and let unconsciousness take him once more.

"He's awake," Cam said, rousing Dr Jay from his sleep. At first, this was confusing, because Dr Jay was pretty sure that he hadn't been awake at all, but then he realised that Cam was talking *to* him, not *about* him.

"Kayode?" he said, lifting his drool-encrusted face from the lab bench. "Kay's awake?"

"Yes. A few minutes ago. Come on."

Dr Jay followed Cam into the morning sunlight and through the quad. He blinked. There was a flash of something behind his eyelids, something that was almost a dream, and he had the feeling that he was grasping for a memory as terrible as it was alluring.

"Is he all right?" Dr Jay asked, a little dazed.

"He's recovering," said Cam. "It might take a while, but he's not as hot as he was and…"

Dr Jay lost the rest of Cam's words as the dream swooped down on him once more, a dream of heat and desire and blood. The feeling of skin soft in his hands, then powdery, then nothing at all.

He looked across the quad, eyes wide with horror and disbelief, but the pile of ashes was still there beside the door, a silent accusation. It hadn't been a dream at all.

Dr Jay stopped walking. When Cam noticed he was no longer following, he stopped too.

"What's up?"

"You need to take me away," Dr Jay whispered.

Cam looked puzzled. "That's what I'm trying to do. We're going to sick bay. Don't you remember?"

He remembered everything.

"That's not what I meant. I meant you need to *lock* me away." As the terrible truth sank in, he finally met Cam's eye. "I'm the reason Kayode's sick, and last night I killed someone. I don't know who. A Silver. He was walking through the college and I just…" He licked his lips, then wished he hadn't because it just reminded him of the blood boiling into his mouth. "You need to take me to see the captain of the Seekers. Now. Please."

Cam looked at him as though he was waiting for the punchline. Then his face fell, apparently realising that the doctor was serious. Deadly serious.

The role of the Seekers was to stop people from exposing the existence of the Silver to humanity, so what Dr Jay had done was not strictly within their remit. However, as he explained to the captain in a hollow monotone, he was so out of control when the urge came over him that he didn't imagine it would be long before he was transgressing all sorts of Silver laws. Regardless, he needed to pay for hurting his dearest friend, and for the life of the man he had taken last night, a man he didn't know and never would now, beyond the taste of his blood.

The interview didn't last long. He told the captain everything that he could remember, which was more and more by each awful second, so much more that he was in tears by the end of it; not of pity, but of self-loathing.

His hubris had brought him here. His stupid arrogance in thinking he could challenge nature without repercussions.

There were only a few of them in Baron Killian Drake's office the next day when he pronounced sentence on Dr Jahan Khalyed for his crimes against the visiting Silver and against Kayode Ladipo. Dr Kay wasn't there – he was still recovering – but Adinde had come along with Cam. Dr Jay didn't know what to say to her, didn't think he had the right to say anything at all, so he kept his eyes fixed on the ground instead.

After considering the evidence, the baron made his decision.

"Burn the notes and bury the serum forever."

"There's none left," Cam said. "There were only two vials, and Dr Khalyed drank them both."

The baron looked over at the corner where Dr Jay sat curled over himself in his seat. "That wasn't quite what I meant."

Adinde's mouth dropped open.

"You can't mean–"

"Do you have another suggestion, Ms Ladipo? The serum is in this man's veins, so he needs to be kept somewhere safe, away from the rest of the Silver. Don't you agree?"

"But *forever*?" Adinde protested. "You can't keep him in a box forever. It would be kinder to kill him."

"Perhaps, but with the chemical assistance he's receiving from the formula, I rather doubt that it would be possible to kill him. Still, I take your point. If you can find a way to render him safe, he may be released in the future."

"I'd rather not be," whispered Dr Jay.

"It's not up to you," Adinde snapped.

And that, apparently, was the end of that. He would be boxed in the baron's basement prison until a cure could be found for the serum. To Dr Jay, it seemed more than fair. For as long as he remained untreated, he was not only dangerous when the hunger descended, but even when he was in control, his body was a walking weapon. A few quick tests performed by Ed had concluded that the serum had bonded to Dr Jay's biochemical make up. It was only luck that had prevented him from burning up when he drank the stuff in the first place. One drop of his blood, or one bite from his teeth, would reduce any other Silver to ashes.

As it had so nearly done to his friend.

All things considered, Dr Jay was happy to be locked away underground where he belonged. He was quiet as Cam led him through the house and down the stairs to the cellar, where a labyrinth of locked doors held back the desiccated bodies of convicted Silver. By the end of the day, one of those doors would bear the name of Dr Jahan Khalyed.

When Cam emerged from the basement alone, he wrapped his arms around Adinde and held her tight. Her husband was Dr Jay's best friend, but Cam knew that she had loved him too. The tears on her cheeks were as much for her own loss as they were for his.

"We'll find a cure," Cam murmured to her. "Ed and Kay between them, they'll find a cure."

"I don't know that they can." She wiped away her tears. "Kay says it's like nothing they've ever encountered before."

"They'll crack it. They always do."

"Not this time, Cam. This time, they just broke it." She breathed out a despairing sigh. "They always leave us to sort out the mess."

Josie Jaffrey is an indie author of urban fantasy, paranormal romance and young adult fantasy who lives in Oxford, England. This short story is a prequel to Seekers, Josie's urban fantasy series. The first book in the series, May Day, features a chaotic vampire detective with a serious grudge against the only man who can help her solve her latest case.

Printed in Great Britain
by Amazon

18428983R00068